SCHOOL FOR SKYLARKS

SAM ANGUS

MACMILLAN CHILDREN'S BOOKS

First published 2017 by Macmillan Children's Books
an imprint of Pan Macmillan
20 New Wharf Road, London N1 9RR
Associated companies throughout the world
www.panmacmillan.com

ISBN 978-1-5098-3959-9

1 3 5 7 9 8 6 4 2

A CIP catalogue record for this book is available from
the British Library.

Printed and bound by CPI Group (UK) Ltd, Croydon CR0 4YY

SCHOOL FOR SKYLARKS

This story is for
Stanley
without whose help it would have been finished in half the time
&
with regrets that there are no whoopee cushions nor
ejector seats to be found in it.

OFF THE EDGE OF THE MAP

Lyla wasn't at all certain that such a house as Furlongs could exist, until she actually had to go there.

'I am NOT staying with Great Aunt Ada.' She spat out the name with precision. 'I'll run away and you won't be able to stop me.'

Father searched Lyla's face as if about to say one particular thing, then thought better of it and said another thing entirely, enunciating with heavy patience.

'London. Will. Be. Bombed. Children. Are. Being. Evacuated.'

'*Some* children are being evacuated, but this one has actually been STOLEN from her bed,' said Lyla through her teeth, tears rising behind her eyes.

Father waited a while, then, with an attempt at levity, said, 'Anyway, you'll enjoy Aunt Ada – she's a little unusual. Do be kind to her.'

'You weren't kind to *Mop*,' snapped Lyla. 'She says you'd've *killed* her with your coldness . . .'

Lyla trailed off – her words, being borrowed from her mother, felt false in her own mouth. Besides, Father being in uniform and about to fight a war made her uneasy and put her somehow in the wrong. She gathered her anger, stoking it so it wouldn't run out of steam. You had to do that because Father's patience was a river that ran on and on, and gave you nothing to push against.

'I've not changed, Lyla. I am the same man I was the day she married me. I loved Mop then, and I still love her now.'

'You left her,' Lyla retorted. 'That's what the papers said. And everyone knows what you did. *Everyone*.' Lyla put on a clipped sort of BBC voice: *'High-ranking civil servant Lovell Spence, cited for infidelity.'*

Father gave a brief, taut laugh. He pushed his foot against the accelerator and the motor swung widely round a tight corner.

'The minute she sees I'm gone, she'll come and fetch me, and if she doesn't I'll escape,' said Lyla.

'Lyla . . .'

He'd been about to say something and then stopped, and Lyla was disappointed because that meant it might, for once, have actually been interesting.

After a while, Father slowed the Austen, sighed, and said with forced joviality, 'I should look around if I were you. You'll need to know where you are to plan your escape.'

Lyla harrumphed and folded her arms tightly in a look-at-me-I'm-upset-and-unfairly-treated sort of way. A solitary ewe grazed along a railway track, and in the distance was what might be a station – a clock, a small pavilion and a sign turned around to confuse the enemy. Lyla scowled. 'It's not as if the Germans would even BOTHER to come to such a faraway place.'

Father inhaled wearily then glanced at his watch. He'd have to drive all the way back to the kind of government meeting that Mop said was always just caution and compromise. The Austen rattled over a cattle grid, then turned between noble gateposts on to an unmade drive. Father slowed the motor, unwound the window and breathed deeply to savour the air.

Just then, the house appeared.

Lyla caught her breath. She saw its crenellations and chimneys, its turrets and swaggering towers. It was baffling, haphazard and rambling, as if all the bits of it had just risen up whenever and wherever they'd wanted, so you couldn't tell for certain where it began and where it ended. Sheep grazed right up to its walls and ferns sprouted from its stones like the plumes of a cavalier's hat. Poetry and romance hung about the turrets and towers, a yearning for the dashing and the untamed that beckoned to something in Lyla's spirit and reminded her of the heroines in the stories she'd read. Nevertheless, she carefully formed an expression of disgust.

'It looks draughty and cold.'

Father chuckled. 'Well, yes – as a matter of fact, it is. When the wind blows, the carpets lift off the floors and dance, the water freezes in the pipes and the cream freezes inside the cows and turns to ice cream.'

'Does it really?' asked Lyla, delighted till she remembered about being cross.

Father pulled up on the circular gravel forecourt beside a door that stood at the foot of a tall octagonal tower. Above its Gothic arch a stone galleon perched everlastingly on the crest of a wave.

'I'm not getting out.'

Father shrugged as if to shake off both the journey and the company of his daughter. He knocked at the door, and immediately it opened and someone appeared – perhaps a butler, for he wore a splendid and ancient livery. He was tall and bore himself with formality and decorum.

'Solomon,' said Father warmly, taking his hands.

'Captain.'

'How are you? How is she, Solomon?'

'Her Ladyship is preparing for war, sir.'

Solomon had the tact and restraint of a butler, but Lyla saw that his eyes twinkled with the faintest hint of amusement.

'Specifically,' he continued, 'she is working on some pyrotechnic illuminations known to herself as Dandelions. They are to confuse the German ships when they steam up the Bristol Channel.'

The twinkle faded from Solomon's eyes, and his face once again assumed the deadpan inscrutability of the butler one might expect to find in such a house as Furlongs. Dipping his head, he withdrew, then walked with a stiff, awkward gait to the luggage on the back of the Austen.

CHOP-CHOP – SHOW 'EM OUT

'Aunt Ada!' called Father.

He stood in a shaft of dust-speckled light cast from a mullioned window. All of a sudden, Lyla saw him for the first time as a person distinct from herself and from Mop. She saw a faraway smile soften and light his face, melting its drawn severity, and she realized she'd never before given any thought to Father's happiness or unhappiness.

She tightened her arms about herself. Mother's unhappiness took up most of the space in Lyla's head, and she had to watch it warily, for at any moment it might suddenly spill and cast its tarry darkness over the day or the week.

Lyla looked about the dim room. Tusks, antlers and medieval weapons hung on either side of the immense stone fireplace. Shields painted in heraldic purples, blues and reds ran around the walls. As Lyla's eyes adjusted, she saw the strangest of things crowded willy-nilly on the hall table: a barometer, the tusks of a walrus and an unnervingly alive-looking armadillo that stood tiptoe on quaint little feet between a tray labelled 'Mail In' and another labelled 'Mail Out'.

'It's just the same, Lyla,' Father murmured. 'Nothing changes here.'

Lyla rolled her eyes. Where was the fun in things staying the same?

Just then, from a low stone arch that led to a low stone passage, a brisk, bright voice called, 'Solomon! Solomon! Where are you, Solomon? There's someone in the place.'

The owner of the voice appeared, wearing an all-in-one sort of outfit – the kind that a fighter pilot might wear, with chest pockets, hip pockets and shin pockets, all of them crammed with pieces of wire and batteries and ticking things. Her eyes were bright and reckless, her skin smooth and clear, but her hair was a startling polar white and roughly sheared as if she'd commandeered a passing groundsman on his way to deal with the brambles. She was quite old, yet she held herself very upright, and there was a vigour to her, the fierce energy of a high-voltage current. On her head perched a pair of goggles and – Lyla took a step closer to make quite sure of this – on her shoulder sat a canary.

She made a shooing motion as if Father were a clutch of hens.

'Show 'em out, Solomon. Chop-chop – show 'em out.'

'Ada, it's me, Lovell.'

Father's voice was warm, amused by Great Aunt Ada's curious brand of hospitality.

'Lovell . . . Oh, good.' She paused for a moment. Then, distracted by the bottle in her hand, she waved it about and said, 'Now, look here, Lovell. Well, d'you see, my Pink Dandelions, they're twenty-four inches diameter – that's a hundred feet wide when they burst, d'you see? They'll do the trick. No, no, I will not fail nor falter in my duty. Invasion will be a matter of life or death for us all.'

Ada had laughing eyes, flecked with gold.

Lyla stepped a little closer to see if the canary on her great aunt's goggles was real or not, but then, seeing that the bottle that her great aunt was brandishing about was labelled 'BLASTING POWDER', she retreated a step or two. Father, however, was smiling.

'Dear Ada, you haven't changed at all. You'll blow the place up one day, you know.'

Ada's attention appeared to have been distracted once again, for now she was unearthing a paper from a pocket and flapping it at Father.

'And this! Number of rooms? Number of acres? Dammit. They won't have it, I tell you. They'll sack the place. Solomon! Solomon! Let no one in! Man the doors!' she said with furious indignation, still oblivious to the fact that her butler was not to hand.

Lyla, tired of being ignored, rolled her eyes. 'Actually,

8

I'm sure Hitler will choose a more comfortable house in a more convenient location.'

'Who's that?' barked Ada, peering in Lyla's general direction, then shaking her head vigorously. 'Oh no, Hitler will never get his hands on the place; the Dandelions – the fireworks – will see to that. No, no, no. He'll be baffled – quite baffled – by my Pink Dandelions when they burst over the Bristol Channel. His instruments of navigation will be befuddled by them, don't you see? Hitler won't know where he is at all and will turn tail, don't you worry. No, no, it's the Ministry of Works – they're the problem – got to keep 'em out, d'you see? They'll turn it into a barracks; fill the place with soldiery and so on, just like the last war.'

Soldiers? Aha! Lyla smiled quietly to herself. If Furlongs was to be filled with soldiers, then she wouldn't have to stay here. Option One: run away. Option Two: request that the Ministry of Works fill Furlongs with soldiers and send her home.

'This is Lyla,' Father announced, attempting to put an arm around his daughter's shoulder.

Great Aunt Ada squinted briefly at Lyla.

'WHO IS SHE?' she roared.

'Did you not get my letter?'

'Plenty of letters, but Solomon knows I don't hold with 'em.'

'Ah, well you must find the letter and read it –

that's important, Ada . . . Lyla's come to stay.'

'I've no intention of staying,' snapped Lyla.

'Lyla,' said Father, 'London will be *bombed*.'

Ada hesitated, then harrumphed.

'Well, I dare say we shan't notice each other much, she and I.'

'You won't notice me at all. Mother needs me, so I'll be returning to London.'

'*Needs* you, you say?' Ada asked with quiet ferocity. '*Needs* you?'

'Yes. In any case, I don't want to be here. You see, I was kidnapped—'

'Two different things entirely,' Ada interjected. 'She needing you and you not wanting to be here. Don't confuse them.'

'I'm not confused at all,' said Lyla promptly. 'Number one – I don't want to be here and have no intention of staying. And number two – Mop will be anxious.'

Great Aunt Ada glanced quickly at Father. Father held her gaze and gave a brief dip of his head. Ada, noting this, paused and then waggled her fingers in a gesture that could be intended to indicate either understanding, dismissal or goodbye – or perhaps all three. Together with her wires and batteries and gelignite she wandered off absent-mindedly towards the corridor, but Lyla, because she did very much want to know, called out after her, 'Is that actually a real canary on your . . . ?' She tapped the top of her head to indicate the goggles that her great aunt wore.

'Ah yes, dear. This is Little Gibson,' answered Great Aunt Ada before continuing off down the corridor on some peculiar business of her own.

'Oh good, Solomon's ready with the motor,' said Father, looking at his watch.

Lyla, abruptly forgetting the matter of the canary being real or not, whirled around in horror. She said nothing, but inwardly as she watched him she was begging, *Don't leave me here! Please, don't just walk away from me.*

'Come, Lyla.' Father went to her and bent to hug her.

Lyla shied away from him but he took both her hands in his. 'Dear Lyla, you've been so very brave.'

She shook her hands free. The blood rose to her cheeks, her fingers clenched and she burned with hurt and rage. *Please don't leave me here. Don't leave me again.*

Father's face creased with pain. 'You are so very loved. You are everything to me.'

Lyla clenched her fists and bowed her head. *He left me once and now he's leaving me a second time.*

'One day perhaps you'll see that I am not so bad a man as you think me now.' With a sigh, Father rose and slowly, head bowed, went out to the motor.

Alone in the hall, Lyla gazed out through the open door and saw him, his hand on the ignition, looking back at Furlongs with a long, sad smile. She heard the engine start and then the scrunch of gravel and she trembled with disbelief and anger. She ran out and stood alone on the gravel and yelled over the splutter of the engine:

'I'll escape, and you won't be able to stop me.'

3

OLD ALFRED

Mop was right. Father was cold: all head and no heart.

Lyla scowled at the weapons and painted shields but saw nothing she could throw or break. Everything was so immense, so ancient and indifferent to her that she felt small and powerless.

She stayed there, alone in the centre of the vast hall, raging and hot and turning about in a welter of rage and indecision. Should she escape now? Right away?

While thinking about her escape, she grew conscious that something or *someone* was watching her.

She looked about.

No one.

She looked about again.

Still no one.

Yet she *was* being watched. She looked about once more and thought it was perhaps the watchful little armadillo on the table. She didn't care what a stuffed armadillo thought of her, not in the least, but she might just turn it around to face the wall.

'Miss – best not to touch Old Alfred,' said Solomon.

Lyla whipped round, and there was Solomon at the foot of the curling stone stairs of the tower. He bore aloft a silver domed platter, and on his face was a gleaming black moustache that curled up at the edges. Lyla grew alarmed – that moustache had *certainly* not been there before. She gawped, but Solomon was so poised and deadpan that Lyla began to wonder if he were a wizard or a magician, or if she perhaps had been bewitched.

She took a deep breath, lifted her hand and held it mid-air, poised between the vigilant armadillo and the inscrutable Solomon. 'All right, I shan't touch *Old Alfred.*'

Solomon walked with his strange, stiff gait towards the stuffed armadillo apparently known as Old Alfred, and, with some panache, placed the platter at his feet, rather in the way that the maître d' at Claridges might present a boeuf en croute. With a flourish he lifted the lid. Lyla watched, astonished. The butler must be as daft as his mistress, for the animal was clearly dead and not in need of any food at all.

'And what food *exactly* does a dead armadillo require?' demanded Lyla.

'Old Alfred is not to be neglected. Those are my instructions.'

Solomon was clearly accustomed to carrying out all manner of things in the line of duty. Lyla watched his face very carefully in case that moustache should disappear or do some other thing.

Suddenly, and rather surprisingly, Solomon bent down and whispered through a smile, 'There is, however, no longer any obligation to rootle about in Her Ladyship's flowerbeds for the bugs and the beetles that Old Alfred so used to enjoy.'

Lyla smiled because Solomon had the sort of smile that always draws a smile in others, and that made her think how lovely it must be to go about seeing only smiles wherever one went. Nevertheless, everything here was strange and absurd. She would go home. She would go home right away and not waste a minute longer.

'Shall I show you to your room, miss?'

'No, because I am going home – and actually I'm going right away.'

Solomon dipped his head, and Lyla wondered if he might have been a little saddened by the idea of her leaving so soon. Lyla glanced out of the hall window and hesitated, suddenly assailed by doubt. The hills were sturdier and the valleys deeper than she'd thought; the drive so long you couldn't see to the end of it.

It would be a tricky journey to London. Wondering if Solomon might try to stop her from leaving, she walked slowly over to her suitcase. Slowly she bent to take the handle, but still he didn't come to stop her. Old Alfred, however, was watching her, *definitely* watching her, as if he knew exactly what she were doing, and had in his life seen all manner of things, and a small girl running away was entirely unremarkable, *see if he cared.*

Lyla stuck her tongue out at Old Alfred, grabbed the handle of her case and turned to find that Solomon was at the door opening it for her. Lyla was disconcerted, for the grown-ups she'd come across in stories did not open doors for children to escape through.

'I'm going to catch the train, and nothing you say will stop me,' she told him.

But Solomon simply conjured a thing from his pocket and held it out in the palm of his hand. A small silver compass.

'From Her Ladyship,' he said. 'To guide you to London.'

Lyla was suspicious and wondered if it were a trick, for grown-ups weren't supposed to help you run away.

'I shan't need it as I'll be travelling by train.'

Solomon dipped his head in the restrained way, which suggested that if he knew any better he also knew it was his place not to disagree.

'Good day,' said Lyla, and marched out.

Halfway down the drive she turned to see if anyone

was watching from the windows or perhaps running down the drive after her, but so far no one was. She turned back and noted again the height of the hills and the depth of the valleys and she scowled, for it was difficult for an eleven-year-old child to return herself to London from a place that was so far away from all the other places in the world. By the time she'd reached the gateposts, her fingers already ached and her tummy rumbled, so she paused to rest. She glanced up at the stone griffins, which were, however, too high up on their posts and too grand to notice Lyla, so she rolled her eyes at them, snatched at the handle of the case and marched on, telling herself, *It's all Father's fault.*

After a while, because her shoes were all wrong and because all suitcases were the wrong shape for being carried, she began to dawdle and to bump and trail the case along the tarmac. Then, after another while, she slumped down on a green verge beside a patch of yellow primroses and sulked. *No one cared about her. No one had even tried to stop her.* She began to yank at the petals of a primrose, snatching them off one by one.

It was so unfair. Everything was unfair. She yanked the petals from another primrose.

The colour yellow plunged Mop into a black mood. Small things could do that to her mother, even things as small as primroses. Perhaps Mop was having a

17

black day today. Lyla bit her lip. On a black day Lyla always stayed close to her mother because she'd be unpredictable, might begin to make lots of calls, and laugh too loudly, then suddenly – and for no obvious reason – begin to cry.

Abruptly, because such thoughts made her uncomfortable, Lyla stood and marched on. The stone banks were so high you couldn't see over them to know where you were, but suddenly she found herself in front of the little pavilion with the platform and the large round clock.

She was halfway home. From now on it would be quite easy.

After a while she looked at the clock and thought how watching clocks made time move more slowly in faraway places. She crossed her arms and legs several times over and looked about, hoping a station master might materialize.

The same solitary ewe grazed along the track as though it lived there always. Uneasy, Lyla gazed down the track, first one way, then the other, wondering from which direction the London train would come, and she gazed at the clock, wondering actually if clock hands moved at all in places such as this. Suddenly, hearing the screech and rumble of an approaching train, Lyla leaped to her feet. It approached at a leisurely pace, toot-tooting until the sheep eventually lifted its head and wandered off the track. Lyla picked up her case in readiness, but now that the track was clear, the train was picking up speed and the driver had perhaps not seen her, so she waved and shouted, and as it picked up more speed, she looked on in disbelief.

The steam gradually cleared and there, emerging from the mist, was Solomon with a pony trap.

'Miss Lyla, just in time for dinner,' he said, and he didn't give any sign that anyone was cross with her, nor show any surprise that the train had not stopped. He dismounted to collect Lyla's case, and she saw again the awkward movement of his legs.

Lyla scowled. She very much liked the idea of being in time for dinner, but because she'd tried to *run away* she must also be cross.

'Why didn't the train stop?' asked Lyla through her teeth.

'This is Her Ladyship's private station, but she has no intention of rushing about on trains.'

'I see,' said Lyla, again through her teeth. Angry tears collected behind her eyes, and blood rose to her cheeks with the rage that comes from having no control over things like trains, or the arrangements that grown-ups made for you in which you had no say. Escape Option One had failed, so now she would have to try Escape Option Two: soldiers and sandbags. She would have to write a letter to the Ministry of Works.

After a while, because Escape Option Two was

actually quite complicated to think about, her mind began to drift, and she noticed that Solomon had no moustache, and because it was disconcerting to have a moustache appear and disappear Lyla wondered whether he might tell her where it had gone and, eventually, she asked.

'Where is your . . . your . . . ?' She made curling actions with her fingers on either side of her mouth.

Solomon turned to her. 'I only put it on to cheer you up, for you looked so sad when Captain Spence left.'

Lyla, unused to such kindness, smiled at him, and as they entered the hall, being by now very hungry, asked, 'What time is dinner?'

'Seven o'clock, Miss Lyla. In the Old Hall,' replied Solomon.

Lyla gestured about the room. 'So what's this meant to be – the *New* Hall?'

Solomon inclined his head. 'Miss Lyla, there are indeed those among us who think this is a rather snappy, up-to-the-minute sort of place. Shall I take you to your room?' He bent to pick up Lyla's case.

'Yes,' she replied. 'I'll probably be leaving in the morning or sometime very soon, but now I do need to go to my room as I've an important letter to write.'

4

WHITE HARES AND UNICORNS

Lyla followed Solomon up the winding stone stairs. They emerged rather suddenly on to a broad landing lined with bookcases and portraits and went a very long way along a corridor flanked with suits of armour.

Solomon paused, and with pride and some sense of occasion announced, 'The Yellow Silk Room, miss.'

Lyla caught her breath. A four-poster bed stood in the centre of the room, richly hung with canary-yellow silk. On the walls, painted unicorns and white hares frolicked between silvery trees whose branches and luminous leaves spread upwards across the ceiling like an enchanted glade.

This was a forgetting kind of room, in a forgetting kind of house, where you might sit about with walruses and unicorns.

Everything was so different to anything Lyla had ever known. She went about with Mop to shops and galleries, restaurants, theatres and concerts, but since Mop disapproved of the countryside ('Mildew, darling – it's all mildew and melancholy'), Lyla had never been further than Henley.

She thought of her mother's delicate furniture and dainty trinkets, and of how Mop was too careful about her appearance to go about in overalls, or leave armadillos in the hall. With a plummeting feeling in her belly, Lyla thought of Mop herself.

After a while she sighed and turned to the window and then her heart missed a beat, for immediately below she saw the high stone wall of what might be a vegetable garden. Walled gardens often appeared in stories she'd read, and she'd always longed to be in one, for they were fairy-tale things; things of promise and plenty; places to fill baskets with pears and plums; places in which to meet secret, special friends and have adventures. Lyla's hopes ran on. Perhaps there'd be a larder somewhere here too, with rows of jellies and jams.

She sighed. She was in fact very hungry, and with hunger came anxiety, for in her experience adults did not always remember to provide food. Mop didn't because her mind was on Higher Things, and that was why Winnie, her housekeeper, had to do the dull bits of life, like meals. Lyla's thoughts had revolved, as they always did, back to Mop. She must return to her, and that meant Escape Option Two, which was filling Furlongs with soldiers.

She went to the spacious writing table on which

stood an ink pen, a silver ink pot and blotting paper, took a sheet of headed paper and began to puzzle over how one went about writing to important men in ministries and finally picked up the pen.

To Whom It May Concern
The Ministry of Works
Horseguards
Westminster

September 1939

She chewed her pen for a while before writing:

Dear Sirs,

I am delighted to inform you that I am willing to make Furlongs and all its grounds available to all the regiments and all the soldiers that may need it. Furlongs is very large indeed and even has several turrets and a butler and a clock tower and would be very suitable for storing sandbags and soldiers.

*Since it would be entirely unsuitable for me to remain in the house when it is full of soldiers, please transport me **at your earliest convenience** to my London residence, 37 Lisson Square, Primrose Hill.*

Yours,

Lyla Spence

Then she added *Lady* in front of her name and smiled, because now the men in government offices would pay special attention and send the soldiers very soon. She would go now and put the letter in the Mail Out tray ready for first post the next morning, and then find her way to the Old Hall by seven, in case Solomon gave her dinner to a dead armadillo known as Old Alfred.

5

WELSH RAREBIT

She found Great Aunt Ada sitting by the fire, her feet propped up on a petit-point footstool, her hands folded across her lap. She wore a brown velvet smoking jacket and slippers embroidered with galleons. Lyla eyed the moth-eaten jacket and wondered if her great aunt dressed herself in the clothes left behind by the previous inhabitant of the house simply because they were readily to hand.

Ada was reading a letter that appeared to be from Father, for it was surely his handwriting, but as Lyla entered she carefully folded the letter and placed it back in the envelope, frowning a little as she did so.

'Good, good,' she said distractedly. 'You are still here. I am so pleased. Do sit down. Violet will be along shortly too.'

Violet? Father hadn't mentioned anyone called Violet. Old Alfred was an armadillo and Little Gibson was a canary so there was no knowing who or what Violet might be at all.

'And this dear fellow is Little Gibson, as you know.'
Great Aunt Ada tapped his beak fondly and handed
him a cuttlebone from the pocket of her mannish
smoking jacket.

The clock struck the hour, and on the seventh
chime exactly Solomon appeared, solemn and
ceremonious and silent.

'Ah, Solomon,' Ada said, as though highly satisfied
that her butler should present himself at that particular
o'clock.

Solomon clearly did the same things at the same
time every day, and probably had done for centuries,
for now he went over to a bookcase, and, with some
pizzazz as if he were a showman about to perform a
trick, pushed it. Lyla blinked furiously, for a section of
the bookcase was swinging open and behind it was a
gleaming silver-domed dish that had perhaps risen of
its own accord from the nether regions of the house.
Solomon placed the dish on the window table.

At an insistent rattling of the window pane, Lyla
was astonished to see a soft pink muzzle at the glass –
the muzzle of a delicate, gentle, soft-eyed horse.

'Good evening, Violet,' said Aunt Ada.

So Violet was a horse. Well, that explained that.

Aunt Ada rose, went to the table and lifted the lid
of the silver platter.

Lyla watched hopefully. *Welsh rarebit. That was good,
but there was only* **one** *portion.*

His demeanour most serious, Solomon turned and opened the casement.

The horse called Violet was so wistful and wise-looking that Lyla felt she might once have been a human who'd been turned into a horse and then cast out and forced, forever after, to peer sadly into the very house in which she'd once lived. That possibility made Lyla feel softly towards Violet, until Violet stretched her neck through the window towards the Welsh rarebit and began to eat.

Dizzy with exhaustion, hunger and astonishment, Lyla felt a tear trickle down her cheek, but she brushed it aside with the back of a clenched fist and said, 'I'll be leaving very soon, you know.'

Lyla knew she'd been rude, but she couldn't help herself.

'Oh dear, your father was so happy here, you know,' replied Ada.

Solomon had returned to his dumbwaiter, and now there were two very promising silver domes, each on a tray with its own salt, pepper and mustard pots. He placed the trays on footstools before the fire and left the room.

Lyla finally ate, savouring the Welsh rarebit, which was very, very good. She heard the hissing and crackling of the fire and began to succumb a little to the enchantment of a house in which a butler served tea to dead armadillos and Welsh rarebit to elderly horses, and began to wonder what sort of conversation one might strike up with a great aunt who lived in such a place in such a way. Eventually she said, 'Sometimes Solomon has a moustache.'

'I believe that is traditional in a lion tamer,' replied her aunt.

Lyla looked bewildered, so Ada elaborated.

'Solomon is from Balham, d'you know – a most unlikely product of that borough. His parents died in a house fire. He was only seven, but he joined a travelling circus, became cage boy to a lion cub.'

Solomon reappeared with a cut-crystal tumbler of whiskey for Aunt Ada.

'Barnum and Bailey. A big top, candy floss, fanfares, roaring crowds – that kind of thing. That's where you got your brio, your pizzazz, isn't that so, Solomon? Yes, yes, by seventeen he was a lion tamer, a great success. He and the lion enacted stories from the Bible; put his head into the lion's mouth, and so forth. Isn't that so, Solomon? Yes, frightfully brave.'

'Roy, my lady. He was called Roy,' said Solomon, his eyes a little misty.

'Quite. Roy. An Asiatic lion, I believe. The jaws of an Asiatic lion can crush the spine of a bull, you know. But then came the war, and Solomon became a soldier-servant – to your father in fact. You know, digging foxholes for Lovell, pressing his uniform, driving him about and so on. Lovell tells me he was very constant, very dependable. And now he's here.' Ada glanced at her butler to denote deep satisfaction that this should be the case. She glanced down at the envelope on her arm rest and drummed her fingers on it. 'Ah well, you see, life takes many twists and turns – puts obstacles in one's way and so forth. One doesn't always end up where one thinks one might.'

'I see,' said Lyla, who'd never known that her father had once had a lion-taming soldier-servant to dig things called foxholes for him.

Great Aunt Ada's house was so far proving most unusual, and Lyla began to look forward to telling Mop all about the things that happened in it. One thing though was a little disappointing, and that was the matter of Old Alfred the armadillo not being alive. So, because she did in fact hope there might be others, she asked, 'Are there any *live* armadillos in your house, Great Aunt Ada?'

'No . . . oh dear, you see, there's only Old Alfred, who was a dear companion, like Solomon – very constant, very dependable. That's what you want: constancy and dependability. These are the things you need in those you choose to love, don't you think? No point at all in wasting time on those who are not constant in their love for you.'

The person Lyla loved was Mop, so she thought about Mop, and then, though she didn't know what to make of Aunt Ada's words, found that they were discomfiting and somehow causing her toast to stick in her mouth a little. She swallowed before chewing it properly, then put down her knife and fork. After a while, she began to speak in a voice that was high and brittle.

'Soon Mop will come –'

Lyla broke off because her words were dissolving, and, unaccountably, tears from deep inside were rising to the surface when she'd had no intention of their doing so. She rose and pushed past Solomon and fled upstairs.

6

DEVILLED KIDNEY

On account of the scratching and peculiar pitter-pattering that went on at all hours of the night at Furlongs, Lyla had not slept well. *Well, she wouldn't be staying long. A plan was in motion. Wheels were turning. The Ministry of Works would send soldiers here, and she would be sent home.*

She rose from her bed, went over to the wardrobe and rifled through her clothes. Someone had done a *very thorough* sort of packing, and Solomon had done an equally thorough job of unpacking. At the far end of the rail was a mothy green cape that wasn't hers. Lyla rolled her eyes. It had probably hung there for at least a century or two.

She went down to breakfast, huffing as she passed a bucket on the stairs, then grinning to think how it probably rained *inside* Furlongs, and how Great Aunt Ada probably sloshed about the place in gumboots. She smiled until she remembered how unfair life was, which made her cross again, that is until the smell of breakfast reached her. A house that held so stalwart a woman as Great Aunt Ada might provide an Empire-Building breakfast of things like eggs Benedict or devilled kidneys.

She paused. There was no Solomon anywhere. She glanced at the Mail Out tray and saw that her letter had gone. Old Alfred was staring at her as if to say, *I know what you are doing. I know about your letter to the Ministry of Works.* So she stuck her tongue out at him, crept to the dining room and peered in.

She glimpsed a splendid table upon which sat enough silverware to host a royal banquet for several heads of state. There'd definitely be toast; perhaps even butter. The door swung open and suddenly Lyla was caught in Ada's cool, bright gaze. Her great aunt was seated at the far end of the table, the canary known as Little Gibson was perched on a toast rack and behind them both stood Solomon, a linen napkin draped over his arm. Ada had newspapers and tea and, indeed, a devilled kidney.

'How marvellous she's still here! We didn't think she would be, did we, Solomon?'

'No, my lady.'

'After all,' continued Ada, 'she's been kidnapped and wishes to return to where she came from.'

Solomon's face remained impassive. His mistress might talk to him, but only under the rarest of circumstances would he venture any opinion of his own.

'Actually I might be here for just a day or two more. But then I must return to London, because my disappearance will be making Mop anxious and worried and upset,' said Lyla.

'I see. Well, I hope you slept well?'

'As a matter of fact I didn't because that room is *haunted*.'

'Ah, but don't you see, it's the person that inhabits it that is haunted, not the room itself,' remarked Aunt Ada, handing a cuttlebone to Little Gibson. 'You bring along the things that haunt you, wherever you go.'

Lyla had no idea what was meant by that. 'Ghosts don't scratch or make noises,' she retorted.

'Oh, but they do. The Green Countess, for example, cries.'

'The Green Countess?'

'She was very, very wicked, and she wore bottle green from head to toe.' Aunt Ada's eyes lit up. 'In fact, the very cape that hangs in your wardrobe belonged to her. And on moonless nights, the door opens and a candle floats across the room—'

Lyla was gawping, until that is, she detected the faintest trace of a smile on Solomon's lips and, knowing then she was being teased, interrupted her aunt. 'Countesses do *not* scratch at floors.'

'Ah, but the scratching is only the mice. You heard mice.'

'Ah, that makes it so much better,' remarked Lyla sarcastically. 'Anyway, it doesn't matter because soon I'll be going home.'

'You won't.'

'I *will*.'

Aunt Ada paused, then tried again. 'Your mother—'

'Needs me,' interrupted Lyla firmly.

As Aunt Ada regarded Lyla with those piercing eyes, colour began to rise to Lyla's cheeks, and her blood started to toss and pitch inside her.

'Just wait! You'll be forced to let me go!' she hissed.

Lyla marched out and stomped up the stairs, keeping to the edges where she'd make most noise, but no one called after her or came running, so at the top she sank down and raged. A short while passed but still no one had come, so she rearranged herself in a noisy, huffy kind of way. Still no one came, so she grew bored and stood and marched past all the knights in armour into the Yellow Silk Room.

Lyla went to the window and waited there all morning, all the fear and anxiety inside her mingling and becoming a physical ache.

If she wished hard enough and kept watching, Mop just might appear, and it was almost as if she were back at the kitchen table in London, gazing out into the street, watching for Mop. If she were in London, Winnie might be at the stove, and if she'd remembered about Lyla's schooling, she might be reciting aphorisms for Lyla to copy out.

Any port in a storm.

A friend in need is a friend indeed.

'Aphorism' was the fanciest word that Winnie ever used, and she was firmly of the view that the *Oxford Book of Aphorisms* contained all the information required to educate a child. According to Winnie, all subjects were covered more than amply by aphorisms. Through the window, Lyla would see other children returning home from school, in happy clusters, holding hands and carrying satchels laden with the sorts of books that Winnie held to have no common sense in them at all.

There was no chance of school or school friends for Lyla because Mop had decided that school hours were most inconvenient, and that, in fact, there was absolutely no need to go to school at all. Actually, you could grow up perfectly well, quite on your own. In fact Mop couldn't remember anything she'd ever hated in her whole life so much as school: school tried to make you into a different shape than the shape you actually were; therefore Lyla must not go to one. And so it was that Lyla's education had been placed entirely in the hands of Winnie and the *Oxford Book of Aphorisms.*

Winnie, placing a pot in a drawer, might say:

A place for everything, and everything in its place.

Lyla would write that down, and Winnie would then say:

Potatoes, three pounds.

And Lyla having duly written that down, would sigh and cross it out, because *Potatoes, three pounds* was probably part of a shopping list. Shopping Lists and Spelling Tests were actually one and the same thing and they went in a different exercise book. By now Winnie, distracted by some dirt on the floor, would have taken up a broom and forgotten all about spelling and shopping and aphorisms, and Lyla would turn again to the window and wonder what other children did at school all day, and she'd watch for Mop and ache for her to return.

As thoughts of Mop flooded Lyla's head she felt her throat constrict. She turned away from the window. Mop would be in a worry and a flurry, for she had a tendency to fluster and to telephone everyone and issue instructions, then to telephone again with counter-instructions, and thus orchestrate a whole whirlwind entirely from the comfort of her bed.

Lyla went to the desk and took a piece of headed paper and paused, thinking that she must be careful not to alarm Mop with news of what had happened.

Furlongs
Ladywood
North Devon

Dearest Mop,

Father has stolen me and DUMPED me in a
faraway-off-the-edge-of-the-world place with Great
Aunt Ada, where there're no taxicabs or anything.
Great Aunt Ada doesn't have a telephone and won't
enter the Modern Age because she doesn't want voices
coming down a line at her just whenever they want
to. In any case the telephone company won't put miles
of cable up for someone who doesn't hold with new-
fangled things. That is why I can't telephone you.

I DID try to escape, but it isn't straightforward.
Trains don't stop unless Aunt Ada tells them to, and
she won't, because trains are also part of the new-
fangled Modern Age, and though she admires them
as a scientist, she has no intention of going about in
them. So if you come and get me, you will have to
come in a motor.

Great Aunt Ada is dotty and there's no getting
through to her about what is important at all, which
is sending me back to London. Her butler is either a
warlock or a sorcerer or a wizard.

37

I do have another Plan in motion so I can get back to you as quickly as possible because I miss you very much, but it is a rather difficult and desperate sort of Plan.

Please don't be worried or get ill. I am all right, but I am worried about you because I've already been here one whole day and you haven't written or come to get me, so perhaps you are having a Black Day? Anyway now my Plan is underway, so hopefully soon I shall be back at home with you.

All my love,

Lyla

7

PERHAPS TOMORROW, MISS LYLA

At Furlongs the same things happened at the same time every day and probably had ever since the beginning of time. Every morning at seven thirty, Cedric Tawny the groundsman would rake the gravel, and his Great Dane, Stephen, always beside him, would watch every stroke and sometimes pounce on the rake and make Cedric smile. Every morning at eight, the postmistress, Mabel Rawle, would cycle up the drive, and Lyla would creep down and peer into the in tray that sat beside Old Alfred in case there was a letter from Mop. Solomon, at the door to the dining room, would see her there, and when she turned, head bowed in disappointment, he'd say gently, *Not today, Miss Lyla*, as though he'd never said it before, and then he'd add, *Perhaps tomorrow, Miss Lyla*.

But on Lyla's seventh morning at Furlongs, Solomon was waiting for her in the hall, an envelope in his hands.

'A letter for you, *Lady* Lyla.'

Lyla sprang towards him, her heart thumping. At last – at last – Mop had written.

Lyla suddenly froze. *Lady Lyla. Not Mop then.* She glanced at Solomon and then at the envelope and noticed now that it was an official-looking sort of letter, not like Mop's elegant stationery at all. She grabbed it and crammed it into her pocket. Feeling a little queasy, Lyla turned and ran up the stairs. *Lady Lyla.* What had Solomon thought about that? She decided she didn't care. Soon the soldiers would be here and she'd go back to London.

Lyla crept away alone to read the letter and found it most encouraging. *The Ministry of Works was most grateful, the nation was most grateful – everyone must do their part in this time of crisis. Large premises in the West Country and all areas unlikely to be targeted by the German bombers were urgently required for the safety of those in urban areas.*

Yes, thought Lyla, *everything was most satisfactory. Everything was going entirely according to plan.*

And yet, somehow, she had begun to feel a little uneasy.

After a while, Lyla shook herself and decided she must explore the house because soon she would be leaving.

First, she decided, she would locate the kitchens and find out if there was a larder full of jellies and jams. So she made her way downstairs and eventually, by following the sound of a wireless, she found the kitchen and a person who must be the cook, for she had a round pink face and a flowered apron and an immense bosom that rested on the surface of a pastry table amidst reams of coloured wool and the only thing that was unexpected about her was the tin hat that was perched on her head.

On the wireless, a man called Mr Middleton was giving instructions about the growing of purple potatoes. The cook was perhaps a little deaf for she was talking very loudly over the sound of Mr Middleton to someone or something – as loudly as if she were shouting into a high wind.

'I got no intention, Henny, no intention of growing none of them things he's talking about, but I do like his personality and I like the way he says "pertaters".'

Who was Henny?

Lyla pushed the door a little wider open. Henny, she could now see, was actually a rather handsome copper hen, which was picking its way along the shelf above the fireplace and looking very well there amidst the copper pans.

The cook waved her knitting about in the direction of Henny.

'All day I have to talk to you – all day or you don't lay. As if I haven't enough on my hands, what with all the jerseys for the merchant seamen.'

After spying for a while on Henny and the cook,

Lyla peered about the kitchen. Then, disappointed because she couldn't see any rows of jellies and jams, she decided instead to find out what Ada did with her days.

She returned to the corridor beyond the library, passing several glass cases housing moths of an especially hairy and horned variety, then came to a door in the middle of which, to her astonishment, was a large letter box, which was an odd thing to see actually INSIDE a house.

'Dotty and moonstruck,' she whispered.

A billiard table stood in the centre of the room, the baize surface strewn with weighing scales, manuals and batteries; tins labelled with 'Ammonal Powder', 'Gelignite', 'Strontium Carbonate', 'Blasting Gelatine', 'Colouring Agent', 'Aluminium Powder' and 'Oxidizer'; wires and detonators; and stacks of what looked suspiciously like very large hand grenades.

I'm stuck in an out-of-the-way place with a very dangerous great aunt, and anything might happen here, thought Lyla.

8

CAULIFLOWER CHEESE

Cauliflower cheese was served every day for lunch, always at precisely one o'clock. Lyla was always hungry by then.

Today, as she entered the dining room, Solomon was waiting at her chair to pull it out, and Great Aunt Ada smiled at her and Solomon said, 'Another letter for you, *Miss Lyla*, in the second post.' He proffered a silver dish with an envelope on it.

Lyla started: if it was another letter from the Ministry, she most definitely didn't want to receive it in front of her aunt. She eyed Solomon and the silver dish warily. *Miss Lyla*, he'd said, perhaps a little teasingly. So probably it was from Mop, and probably it was to say she was coming to take Lyla back to London.

'Oh, I knew Mop would write soon,' said Lyla, reaching for the envelope.

'Did you?' Great Aunt Ada's bright gaze rested on her.

Lyla suddenly saw her father's writing on the envelope. She drew her hand back and, blinking fiercely, said, 'Actually, perhaps her letter has got lost.' She looked down. Solomon waited with the envelope, but tears were brimming in Lyla's eyes, so she snatched up her knife and fork to look as if she had other things to do than worry about letters.

Aunt Ada enquired of her butler, 'Solomon, it is from Lovell, is it not?' At Solomon's nod she continued, 'Yes, child, from your father. You must read it.'

'No. I don't want any letters from him. Ever. I shall never read anything he writes.' *Why hadn't Mop written? Why did it have to be from Father?*

There was silence for a minute. Solomon withdrew a step or two.

After a while, Great Aunt Ada said quietly, 'You are all your father has.'

'He walked out on us,' retorted Lyla. 'That's what the papers said. And everyone knew. *Everyone.*' Lyla put on her BBC voice. '*High-ranking civil servant Lovell Spence, cited for infidelity.*'

'I see,' said Ada, watching Lyla attentively. 'He was unfaithful, was he, Lyla? Did your mother tell you that?'

'Captain Lovell Spence, cited for infidelity,' chanted Lyla once more, with bitter sarcasm. 'No one had to tell me anything.' Perhaps she needed to explain things more clearly to her aunt, who had lived so long in the country that she knew nothing of the world. 'If you're cited for infidelity, it means you've been unfaithful and you've walked out, and so a divorce has to happen.'

'Poor Lovell – he is too much a gentleman . . .'

Why was Great Aunt Ada so dim? She got it all wrong.

'A perfect gentleman, always, my lady,' said Solomon with warmth.

Solomon was dim too. They were both dim and both completely wrong.

Lyla looked up and snapped. 'No, not poor Father. Poor Mother. Poor me. *He* walked out on *us. He* did it—'

'Lyla, when a man is a gentleman, it is often he in a court of law who—'

Lyla clapped her hands to her ears, cutting her aunt short. 'That's not true.'

Aunt Ada watched Lyla, and eventually, as if taking a gamble, said, 'I know, Lyla. I tell you what – if you're really, really sure he walked out on you and your mother, *really* sure, you certainly don't want to read his letter, do you?'

Lyla moved her head from side to side. *No, I don't want his letter*, she told herself.

'Oh dear, well, this is all rather sad, isn't it, Solomon?'

Solomon bowed his head and did in fact seem very

45

sorry about the whole business of Lyla not wanting to read the letter.

But Ada continued, her voice bright and brusque. 'Well, what shall we have, Solomon, a Spitfire or a Vickers Wellington?' She turned to Lyla. 'Solomon is rather clever at fighter planes, he can even do Sopwith Camels – they were from the last war, you know.'

Solomon, very upright and serious, answered,

'The Supermarine Spitfire Mk II, madam.'

Suddenly her Great Aunt Ada's butler was opening the letter from her own father and unfolding it and placing it on the table and smoothing it down, then swiftly, deftly, folding it a different way, folding again and again, and Lyla was watching, most impressed.

'Yes, yes, Solomon has many skills. Lions, planes, foxholes. D'you see, he's a man of infinite parts.' She watched Lyla, and Lyla, a little uncomfortable, watched the butler fold her father's letter with swift, concise movements into a most accomplished aeroplane.

'Open the window, Lyla,' commanded Great Aunt Ada.

Still more uneasy, Lyla rose and went to the window.

'Solomon you were seven, were you not, in that house fire?' asked Aunt Ada.

Solomon gave a brief nod, then, applying the same formality and sense of ceremony to the launching of a Supermarine Spitfire as to all duties, stretched his left

46

arm ahead and, taking aim, drew his right arm back.

Ada turned to Lyla.

'So you see, he's never had a father to write him letters, unlike you.'

Solomon paused and glanced at Lyla, and Lyla saw that he was reluctant about firing the letter plane, but she nodded a determined *get on with it* to him, and, a little sadly perhaps, he turned and launched the Supermarine Mk II Spitfire, sending it straight and true through the window and out over the knot garden where it was caught in the tangled branches of the old damson tree.

'That's what we do with letters we don't want, isn't it?' said Ada, turning to Lyla.

'Yes,' whispered Lyla, glancing out and seeing how the letter, caught on a twig, looked frail and small as a songbird. She bit her lip – then in a determined voice added, 'Because he doesn't love me.'

9

THE SUPERMARINE SPITFIRE MK II
IN THE DAMSON

My darling Lyla,

*I have received orders to leave for France tomorrow.
I am older than I was and my role in this war will
be very different to that in the last. It is unlikely I
will find myself in the front line fighting this time,
and, on account of my languages perhaps, I have
been recruited for some rather shadowy work, a kind
of undercover intelligence gathering – so sometimes
I may find myself unable to write to you. Therefore,
should you ever think of me (I know it may be some
while perhaps before you do), do not be alarmed if you
do not hear from me for long periods of time.*

*How I will miss having dear Solomon at my side,
as chauffeur, runner, valet, as I did in the last war.
Solomon, of course, was hit in the leg and will never
serve again, though he is the younger of us.*

This will be a nasty war. Poor Poland is caught between Germany and Russia. Hitler will invade Britain, and London will be badly hit. Our prime minister is a blind man and a fool, and Germany a dangerous enemy.

Darling Lyla, I am so glad to think that you will be safe at Furlongs, with Ada and with Solomon.

Yours always,

Father

BUCKET

That night when Lyla went up to bed, she found as usual that her lamps were lit, her covers turned down, and the Yellow Silk Room cosy again in the way that seemed designed to make her feel ungrateful.

To make her feel doubly ungrateful, tonight there was a new detail. On her pillow sat an interesting-looking wicker fishing basket tied with a blue ribbon and and a label.

> *His name is Bucket.*
> *He'll be good for keeping mice at bay, Love Ada.*

It's a bit awkward to be given something by someone you've been plotting against, so Lyla yanked sulkily at the ribbon. The basket lurched and Lyla started at a squeal and a hissing that was followed by an alarming slithering inside that rocked the basket to and fro.

In such a house as Furlongs, where the butlers were paper-plane-making-lion-tamers and the great aunts went about with gelignite, there could be no knowing what unpredictable, unknowable kind of creature that was good for keeping mice at bay might be inside a basket, but after a while Lyla's curiosity got the better of her caution. She lifted the lid and saw a small nose and bright eyes and the pale cinnamon face of a young ferret. She lifted the lid a little more and saw a fluffy feather-boa kind of tail.

Bucket put his tiny forepaws on the rim of the basket, placed his snout between them and twitched it and twitched it again.

Lyla gazed at him, enchanted, and whispered, 'Hello. I'm Lyla.'

She placed a finger on his snout and ran it back to the tip of his head, and then, because Bucket didn't make any intimidating snarling noises, she ran it further down his back. He remained still, and, with a nervous, cat-like caution, seemed to assess the quality of her character before making up his mind about her.

'I'm quite all right, you know,' Lyla whispered sadly, a little defensive. 'In fact, there's not much wrong with me at all. It's only that I was stolen from Mother when she was sleeping, so now I'm in the wrong place.'

She ran her fingers along his sinuous spine once more, and gradually he began to purr and his tail grew full and bushy. After a while he placed his snout in the palm of her hand and crept, one tiny paw over

11

LAUNDRY BASKETS

For the next few days, Lyla wandered about from place to place, coddling Bucket and whispering to him. Bucket was a very gentle creature really. If he was happy, he would lie around Lyla's neck; and if he was scared, he needed urgently to be somewhere dark and would scuttle up the sleeve of Lyla's jersey. Lyla had discovered how much more fun it was to do things if you had someone to do them with. Nevertheless, she was worried about Mop and decided she must write to her.

> *Furlongs*
> *Ladywood*
> *North Devon*
>
> *Dearest Mop,*
>
> *The only good thing is that now I have a friend called Bucket. He is my first real friend and I am going to*

take him everywhere I go and when I come to London, which will be soon, you will meet him. He is a very naughty ferret. Last night I had to put him in my sock drawer because he twitches and whines so much when he is dreaming of mice. When he wakes up he has to do a great deal of yawning and stretching. He keeps escaping and hiding in laundry baskets and shoes and does wicked things like taking all the feathers out of pillows though Great Aunt Ada says she doesn't give a hoot about pillowcases and cushions and things, that they're there to be used as one pleases. All because of Bucket I don't have any socks left nor any stuffing in my pillows – but he is my only friend here.

Furlongs is actually quite a fun sort of place. I don't think you would like it because it is quite still and nothing ever changes, and I know you like change and to be in a whirl and to plan for every minute of every day because that keeps away your melancholy . . . but sometimes I think it could even be quite nice to stay here if it weren't for your being so far away.

Great Aunt Ada is either very, very clever or very, very dotty. She keeps gunpowder and cordite in the Billiard Room and is very likely to blow the house up, so it is unsafe and I might die because she is unpredictable – there's no knowing at all what she'll do next, and her butler is a lion tamer, so there's no knowing what he'll do next either – but he does love Aunt Ada very much and is a devoted servant.

Anyway, I hope my plan is working and I hope I can come home soon, but if I don't, PLEASE, PLEASE, DON'T FORGET ABOUT ME. DON'T LEAVE ME HERE FOREVER.

All my love,

Lyla

12

THE RED LIBRARY

Lyla had decided that she and Bucket must explore the room Solomon called the Red Library, because libraries tended to be magical, secret places in which anything might happen.

She crept in and gazed around her. The books went all the way around the walls and up to the ceiling on all sides, so you would need to be a monkey to get to the top shelves, but Lyla spied a set of library steps with castors and grinned at Bucket. Wheels were just the thing, so she climbed the steps and began to propel them both up and down the length of the room. Bucket didn't think much of this kind of transport at all and scuttled up her sleeve in horror, but Lyla, grinning, continued regardless, running a finger along all the spines as she went.

The first book she stopped at was *The Homemade Projectile*, and the next, *The Primary Explosive*. Since those titles were a little unnerving, Lyla gave up on books and went over to the globe that stood in the mullioned window. She twirled it with the tip of her finger and watched all the tiny islands of the world spin by, wondering which small and sandy one she could go to live on one day with Mop.

'Mop and I will go to . . .' She shut her eyes tight as the globe spun and wished for somewhere that had monkeys and mangoes. She stopped the globe, opened her eyes and read aloud, 'Baffin Island . . .' She frowned. 'We'll go to Baffin Island . . .' And then because she couldn't think what you might do on Baffin Island, for it looked a white and cold sort of place, she spun the globe again and whispered, 'After Baffin, we'll go to . . .'

This time she kept her fingers on the warm, middle part of the world, and when it stopped spinning she read, 'Hummingbird Island.'

She wondered if Hummingbird Island was a hard-to-get-to-small-and-faraway place, and then she began to wonder if it was nearly cauliflower cheese o'clock, because globetrotting was hard if you found yourself on Hummingbird Island but didn't know what sort of things happened there, and she was about to give up when she heard the sound of motors.

She crept to the window, peered out, yanked the curtains closed, retreated in alarm, then peered out once more just to make sure.

Two motorcars had pulled up on the gravel, the official black sort that set her pulse racing.

The men from the Ministry were here. The soldiers were on their way.

The sort of men that inevitably travelled in those sorts of motorcars had gathered on the forecourt and were gazing up at the windows and towers. Watching them, Lyla suddenly felt very small and not at all like a Lady Lyla. Then, with a flash of inspiration, she raced upstairs, tore into her room, grabbed the cape Ada said had belonged to the Green Countess and slung it about herself. She looked in the glass. The cape had been out of date for a century or more, but Men from Ministries wouldn't know that. She tugged the hood so only her chin was visible and then took Bucket from his basket and put him on her shoulder. Bucket rather approved of the cosy hood of the cape and arranged himself rather fetchingly about her neck like the fur stoles that countesses probably wore all the time, and Lyla decided that the whole effect was most grown-up-making and was very satisfied.

She rushed downstairs, for she must get to the door before Solomon. At this hour he would probably be in the pantry, but you could never tell, for he was most punctilious about things like opening doors.

13

LADY LYLA

From the balustraded Gallery overlooking the Painted Hall she saw the men from the Ministry of Works huddled together below, looking about, awestruck as tourists in a cave of stalactites. She lifted her head and, taking care not to trip on her skirts, went down the stairs. As she went, she tried to think of grand and grown-up-sounding things to say. By the time she got to the bottom, she'd thought of so many that she determined she must get them all out quickly, before they got muddled, because words had a habit of doing just that when you most needed them.

'Lady Lyla?'

'Well, actually no, that is, yes and no,' Lyla said in a tumbling rush. 'But in fact, Furlongs is quite ready and quite suitable for your needs and you may take possession immediately. I shouldn't think they'll mind at all about the ghost or the mice or the milk that freezes inside the cows, but you must please tell them to take great care of my elderly relative – she is most delicate and I doubt she'd survive in any other place and they must feed her devilled kidneys at eight, cauliflower cheese at one and Welsh rarebit at seven.'

This being the very first instant that Lyla drew breath, one of the men stepped forward and said with some urgency, 'We're here to assess the safety of the Tudor Undercroft for a gymnasium—'

'Undercroft?' interrupted Lyla. She bowed her head as if to consider the suitability of the Undercroft – deciding such a place, if it existed at all, was probably a damp sort of cellar – and said, 'Oh no, probably not at all suitable. They'll get damp in their bones and mildew on their uniform and arthritis in their knees.'

'Ah, well, we could perhaps allow the headmistress to make up her mind about that.'

'Headmistress?' asked Lyla, a sea-sicky swell forming in her belly. 'What *kind* of headmistress?' To her knowledge soldiers didn't require headmistresses nor, for that matter, gymnasiums.

'Did you not receive our letter?'

Lyla wondered if there'd been a second letter that Solomon had perhaps intercepted.

'Letters go *astray* in this house; they're turned into aeroplanes,' she said quietly.

Then, because she had to know, she asked again, 'What *kind* of headmistress?'

The men glanced at one another, and one of them inspected a clipboard very closely and answered, 'Miss

Pinnacle, the Headmistress of Garden Hill School for Girls.'

'Garden Hill School for Girls,' echoed Lyla, nauseous. Her hand rose to Bucket and she stroked him anxiously. A *school*? If a school came to Furlongs, what would happen to her? Would she have to go to it? Would the men from the Ministry perhaps not return her to London at all? Besides, there was Great Aunt Ada to consider. She wondered if it were possible to conceal a headmistress and an entire school from her great aunt for the duration of the war. Plumping for the negative, she began to burble.

'The Undercroft is old and below ground and therefore entirely unsafe and on no account must anyone use the ground floor nor the first floor, nor in fact any floor because all the upper floors are unsuitable. There are buckets in simply every room and bats in every wardrobe, naked Greeks in the Orangery and knights in armour in the corridors, so you see the whole house is quite, quite unsuitable. Garden Hill girls are probably delicate and unused to lion tamers and armadillos and they'll get consumption or develop nervous dispositions.'

'Lady Lyla, I'm afraid,' said another man, 'they're arriving shortly' He glanced outside. 'In fact, they'll be here any minute.'

'Well, we must decide what to do with them, must we not?'

Aunt Ada's voice was a foghorn, a gong and a church bell all in one, and coming down, as it did, from the Gallery, it was as if a thunderclap had spoken, and now they were all staring up at Great Aunt Ada, and her goggles, overalls and canary. All, that is, except Lyla, who pressed herself against the wall and hissed, 'As you see – she's quite delicate – very delicate.'

At the sound of approaching vehicles, all those in the hall turned to see a cavalcade of lorries and buses heading determinedly past the bracken and the sheep.

14

A STEEPLE

Lyla, glued to the window, stared in fear and envy at the unending stream of girls in burgundy uniform that disembarked from the buses and gathered on Great Aunt Ada's forecourt. Great Aunt Ada, however, eyed, with a sort of scientific curiosity, the desks, lockers, beds, pianos and blackboards that were accumulating on the gravel.

She turned to Lyla. 'Your escape plan, I take it? Most impressive. Resourceful. Imaginative. Determined. All most commendable. Besides, in fact, rather a relief. Schoolgirls are so much cleaner and more orderly than soldiers.'

Lyla stared at her great aunt. It was in fact a relief to her too that Ada should take the invasion of Furlongs by hundreds of schoolgirls so much in her stride, but that was the *only* upside to the circumstances, because she didn't know anything about girls of her own age nor what they did or learned or thought or talked about.

Solomon appeared and ran to the window, then turned to Great Aunt Ada, ready at her command to bar the door, hold off all intruders, to defend his mistress and her house to the last. 'My lady—'

Great Aunt Ada held out a hand to restrain him.

Then the cook appeared from the kitchens and peered out cautiously from the top of the stone stairs, still in her flowered apron, her face still very pink. She took another step, gazed out of the window, then threw her hands up,

'The last straw, that is. I'm not feeding all that lot. I got enough on my hands what with all them merchant seamen bein' so cold and me knitting for them every hour God gives me.'

Aunt Ada turned to her and said, 'Dear Prudence, do stop that. The merchant seamen shan't mind at all if you don't send them any more jerseys. Do take her back downstairs, Solomon.'

'Yes, my lady.' Solomon approached to shepherd Prudence away.

Lyla crept to the stone stairs, climbed a couple of steps to the arrow slit and stood on tiptoe to peer out. The girls wore burgundy blazers, stripy ties, grey pinafore dresses and straw boaters. Lyla's hands flew to the fastenings of the ancient green cape. She let it fall about her and hurriedly kicked it under the curtains, but since Bucket was so cosy and sleepy she left him where he was.

The girls were forming pairs and falling into lines, all the while gazing up at the walls of Furlongs in astonishment and wonder. Through narrowed eyes, Lyla saw their long socks and decided that they were probably quite prickly and that she'd quite happily never ever wear socks like that nor a dress that swung from side to side. She saw that they whispered to each other and wondered what sort of things schoolmates said to one another. She saw too that some were holding hands, and that made her a little sad for – never having been to school herself – her only friend until Bucket arrived had been Winnie.

Solomon reappeared with the china and the silver candelabra and dust sheets to move one part of Furlongs to another. Ada saw him and sighed.

'Really, Solomon, what has got into you? They're not vandals come to sack the place – they're schoolgirls.'

Alone at the window, Lyla absently toyed with the hem of her cape, wondering if perhaps burgundy was actually a nice colour, even if Mop didn't like it. Perhaps Lyla was more school-shaped than Mop because there was something about all the Garden Hill girls wearing the same colour and doing the same thing at the same time that looked actually quite fun.

Hockey sticks, pianos, pots, pans, ink-stained desks, tattered chairs, lockers, bedheads, blackboards, and all manner of unlikely things now surrounded the fountain, and in the midst of it all, high-up hair like a steeple that might direct you to a righteous place, was a small, shrill woman with the voice of a town crier. That must be Miss Pinnacle, Lyla thought, and because Miss Pinnacle looked so fearsome, she instantly decided that perhaps, like Mop, she wasn't so school-shaped after all.

Once she'd marshalled her girls into lines, and the desks and chairs were piled up like stacks of ammunition, Miss Pinnacle raised her staff and strode across the forecourt as if to stage an assault on the inhabitants of the place. Lyla saw the mellow, worn stone of Furlongs, and thought of its towers and turrets, and feared that all their romance and mystery would shrivel and shrink away in the face of this alarming woman.

There came a brisk and militant rapping at the door, and Lyla waited in nervous enthralment for the collision of this person and Great Aunt Ada.

15

GREAT AUNT ADA'S PISTOL

The door swung open and Miss Pinnacle swept into the room, her black gown billowing behind her. She had at some point perhaps mislaid her chin, for her head was all nose-shaped, with a small, round mouth and a backwards-sloping forehead that brought to mind dry bread and penitence.

Lyla glanced down at Miss Pinnacle's shoes, for Mop said shoes were a clue as to character. They were the heavy lace-up kind that indicated sound sense and very little else. Following Miss Pinnacle was a lumpy sort of girl with an indecisive chin and a yellow badge, and it seemed to be her job to carry the headmistress's files about.

Miss Pinnacle's eyes settled on Lyla and she started, as if astonished to find anyone in the place. Then, recovering, she looked Lyla up and down and said peremptorily, 'I was at no point informed that there'd be a child on the premises. You will of course have to attend my school.'

Lyla, fearing Winnie's schooling wasn't up to the level of Garden Hill for Girls, replied, 'Certainly not. Number one, I don't believe in school. And number two, I'll be returning to London very soon.'

'Your name?' Miss Pinnacle demanded.

'Lyla.'

'Lyla what?'

Lyla hesitated before whispering, 'Spence.'

'Spence . . . Spence . . .' Miss Pinnacle pondered on this as if trying to remember something. 'Well, I, Miss Pinnacle, known to my girls as The Pinnacle, am the headmistress of Garden Hill School for Girls. Now . . . let me see –' she unfurled some papers – 'We shall be occupying the State Rooms, the Undercroft, the North and South Galleries, the Long Room, the Library –'

She stopped abruptly as though a sudden thought had come to her.

'*Spence*, you said?'

Lyla, growing uneasy, nodded.

'And your parents?'

'Lovell Spence is my father.'

'Your mother's name?'

Some instinct made Lyla pause before whispering, 'Florence.'

'Florence Spence . . . Oh dear . . .' The Pinnacle withdrew a step or two. 'Quite – I thought as much. Well, mercy and grace are my watchwords; I won't visit the sins of the parent on the child. Come,' she said, grasping the bewildered Lyla by the elbow.

Bucket, disgruntled at being so rudely disturbed from his sleep, arched his back and bared his teeth. The Pinnacle gulped and stepped back as Lyla's fur stole appeared to come to life. Noting the presence of a new person about the place, Bucket's tail grew thick as a bottle brush, and he let out a hiss.

Eyeing the hissing ferret from a safe distance, Miss Pinnacle recovered her poise, lifted her chin and said, 'You, child – you will no doubt benefit greatly from all Garden Hill has to offer. Yes, we shall bring you into line in no time at all.'

'You shall do no such thing. There's nothing wrong with her as she is,' boomed Ada.

The Pinnacle turned from the hostile ferret to Ada and paused. Slowly she absorbed the apparition that was Lyla's great aunt, starting in surprise as she took in the goggles and overalls and canary and all the various, unexpected elements of Ada, a series of gulps proceeding visibly down her body as if she'd swallowed a bible or some other uncomfortable thing.

'And what are *you* doing here?' she enquired once she'd recovered her power of speech, glancing once more at Little Gibson to make quite certain there was, in truth, a small yellow bird perched upon a pair of goggles.

'What's this? I can go where I like.' Ada drew

herself up. 'I am Ada Spence, and this has been my family home since the Norman Conquest.'

The two women locked eyes in bewilderment that there could be such a creature in existence as the other, and in both their eyes was the glint of battle, silent and ferocious.

The first to be discomfited by this deadlock was The Pinnacle, who, taking a deep and visible breath, also drew herself up and said, 'I see. And are you intending to remain here?'

Great Aunt Ada strolled to the table, collected *The Times*, sauntered across the room and plumped herself down in a deep armchair, slinging her feet on to a footstool. 'My house has been generously offered to the nation for the duration of the war, and for that you have to thank my great niece.' Ada glanced at Lyla. 'However, Furlongs is, as I have already said, my own home, and has been since the eleventh century, and I shall do as I like in it, when I like, for as long as I like.'

'Of course,' The Pinnacle said tightly. 'But we must all endeavour to be an example to the girls, must we not?' She raised her brows as she formed the question, and her eyes settled on Little Gibson. 'In the meantime, perhaps you'll direct me to the State Rooms?'

Ada shook open *The Times* and, eventually, spoke from behind it.

'Climb fifty stairs and bear north-east. Since Mercy and Grace are your watchwords, and since you seem confident you've all the company of heaven on your side, you'll have no difficulty finding your way, Miss Pinion.'

'Pinnacle.'

'Quite, Pinnacle.'

The Pinnacle tightened her lips and lifted her nose-shaped head heavenwards and barked, 'Put these in position, Mary,' to the yellow-badged book-carrier, handing her a sheaf of what looked like arrows and signs. 'Mary Masters is my head girl.'

The officious and self-important Mary Masters immediately began to busy herself taping yellow arrows and signs to Ada's ancient walls.

IVth FORMERS TO THE NORTH GALLERY

ART DEPARTMENT TO THE ORANGERY

Lyla looked on resentfully at the head girl, who was making herself so at home in Great Aunt Ada's house. But Ada simply continued to read *The Times* and appeared not in the least concerned what might take place in the various rooms of her house, leaving the faithful Solomon to worry about all the delicate and precious things that must be protected.

FRENCH TO THE STATE DINING ROOM

DOMESTIC SCIENCE TO THE LAUNDRY

'French? Hogwash. Domestic Science? Poppycock,' remarked Ada from behind *The Times*. 'Pintuck is intolerable, Solomon – d'you hear me? Intolerable.'

Lyla shrank away, squirming that her aunt should speak in so many decibels just when the Garden Hill girls had begun to enter, two by two, each carrying a chair and pausing to look around the hall, astonished.

'We're at *war*, Solomon,' growled Ada, 'make no mistake. Pinhole and I are at war. Bring me my pistol.'

'Of course, my lady,' said Solomon. He bowed and withdrew, together with the porcelain urn he was carrying.

Lyla began to wonder about Great Aunt Ada going around with a pistol, until a still more alarming thought occurred to her. She crept down and hissed from behind the curtain, 'I won't have to go to the school, will I?'

Aunt Ada lowered *The Times* and lifted her disconcerting gaze to her niece.

'You will. Since you have invited them, they are your guests, and you will attend all classes. I will have a word with Pinion on the matter.' Her eyes sparkled. 'However, on no account are you to allow the teachers to stop you being you.'

Other members of staff entered now, whiskery, talcum-powdery women, smelling of lily of the valley and violet creams, and afterwards came an excitable stream of girls bringing with them into the Painted Hall lockers and hockey sticks, lumpy pillows and chairs and chalkboards, and all the while the first girls to enter were already rushing back downstairs, high-spirited and disorderly.

Solomon handed something wrapped in a handkerchief to Great Aunt Ada, and Lyla eyed it as she slipped it into one of her many pockets. 'What will you do with that pistol?' she asked her aunt.

'Oh, I don't know – I might just shoot Pinpoint,' mused Ada aloud. 'On the other hand, there's a WAR on, and we must be prepared . . . Now, listen here, Solomon, I'm sounding the retreat,' she announced. 'Temporarily, mind you. My living quarters will be the Smoking Room, my HQ the Billiard Room, and Prudence maintains Absolute Control of the Kitchens.'

The last of the girls were entering now, and at the end of them all came one final, solitary girl, her hands on her head.

'Catherine Lively, where is your chair?' Mary Masters asked the girl.

The girl called Catherine Lively looked up.

'I found it impossible to carry a chair while keeping my hands on my head. If you can do it, I'd like you to show me how it's done,' she answered.

Lyla grinned, fascinated. *Catherine Lively*. Mary Masters pursed her lips,

'Well, perhaps you'll think harder next time you decide to make up nasty rhymes about your elders and betters. Hands off your head. Fetch a chair.'

Mary turned to pin a sign to the oak newel post of the Great Stairs. Catherine Lively removed her hands from her head and, as Mary turned her back, caught Lyla's eye and whispered something that sounded very like, 'Mary Mary Unnecessary.'

The last of the girls were rushing on excitedly up the Great Stairs, and Catherine Lively turned to fetch a chair.

IVth FORMERS TO THE CHINESE BEDROOM

Lyla froze. Mary might have another sign about the Yellow Silk Room! But that room was hers and no one else's, and no Garden Hill girl was going to take it away from her. Hoards of Garden Hill girls might at just this minute be arranging their horrid iron beds and saggy mattresses and lumpy pillows in there among her hares and unicorns.

NO ENTRY

Lyla raced up the curling staircase, heart pounding, and ran full tilt down the corridor, but when she reached the West Wing she found all was quiet. She slowed as she went along the corridor, listening intently, but all appeared to be as it should. She burst into her room, rushed to the desk, grabbed a pen and wrote in furious capitals:

NO ENTRY
VERY, *VERY* PRIVATE

Lyla crept out and tacked the note to the door. She paused, listened, then went back in, restless and wondering what to do next. As she thought about the girls, something began to prey on her mind: if she were to join the school, she would need a uniform. Until she had one, it was really rather awkward being in a different-coloured dress to everyone else. There might, just might, be something grey in the wardrobe, though it was unlikely. Mop didn't approve of grey, but Lyla quickly rifled through her clothes just in case.

Nothing.

Anyway, she didn't want to join their classes, and so it would be IMPOSSIBLE to remain at Furlongs a minute longer. *She must escape.*

She grabbed the pen again.

Furlongs
Ladywood
North Devon

Dearest Mop,

THIS IS VERY URGENT.

Things have got even worse because, instead of the soldiers, a whole school of girls has come and it is horrid because hundreds of them are going about whispering and giggling and they might steal my room or sleep in my bed.

What is most annoying is that Great Aunt Ada doesn't mind at all about a school being here, because in the other war she had soldiers and they were noisier and dirtier than schoolgirls, and what is even more terrible is that I have to do lessons and be a part of the school but I don't have any uniform so I will stick out and I won't understand anything of what they do in lessons.

The head girl is called Mary Masters, and I already know that I don't like her at all. But there is a girl called Catherine who makes up rhymes and she might be a fun person to be friends with.

Please don't leave me here forever, as I do so much want to be with you, and every day I wait for a letter from you but it never comes.

All my love,

Lyla

17

A SURBURBAN SOUL

Lyla found that she felt self-conscious about being all alone when she could hear the footsteps and whispering of girls her age, so she decided she must come up with another plan of escape. Her plans so far had not exactly had the right outcome, but she would keep trying. So she sat at her desk and put her head in her hands to concentrate, but after a while a thing kept coming into her mind that was not at all about Escape Option Three but about the way in which the Garden Hill girls were arranging their beds. Were they so close together they could whisper from one bed to another? That was what Lyla wanted to know.

Lyla crept to the North Wing, dawdling in the corridor in such a way as not to appear that she might be heading to the Gallery. Hearing footsteps filing towards her, she slipped into a housemaid's cupboard, and from there she glimpsed the girls' swinging skirts and shining shoes. When they'd gone, she crept up to the Gallery and peered in. A line of beds ran down the room, a gas mask draped from the foot of each, the sheets crisp, the blue candlewick bedspreads turned neatly down. Between each bed was a single wardrobe.

Towards the far end of the room two girls were bent over a bed, whispering as they tucked in the sheets in tidy hospital corners. One of them was Catherine Lively.

'Imelda, don't you think this house is rather fun? So full of peculiar things.'

'Very peculiar. I'm sure we won't notice them at all after a bit, nor that weird aunt person who lives here,' said Imelda, who had colourless, wispy hair.

Indeed, Lyla thought, indignant on behalf of Ada and of Furlongs.

'Imelda Pole Suburban Soul,' chanted Catherine.

'You'll have to put your hands on your head again if you keep making up rhymes that annoy people, Cat. Anyway, you don't think we'll have to stay here for the *whole* of the war, do you?' asked Imelda.

'I think we're lucky to be here at all *actually*.'

Cat, thought Lyla. *I like Cat. If I was absolutely forced to talk to any of them, I would talk to her.*

18

MORNING PRAYER

The sound of the assembly bell the next morning was followed by the rattle of feet and then by a singing that filled the halls and corridors of Furlongs. Lyla would be late. She crammed on the yellow jersey with the sleeves that Bucket had taken to, but then she paused and went to the mirror. Yellow was really awkward if everyone else was wearing burgundy. Lyla's hands rose to her hair to tidy it. She stared at herself some more, wondering what it might feel like to wear a grey dress with a swinging skirt.

She sighed, turned and went to the sock drawer for Bucket and tickled him till he woke. He stretched and yawned and stretched some more. Lyla coaxed him into her sleeve, then crept out towards the landing. She peered down and saw the girls ranged on the stairs: the youngest at the foot by an upright piano, the bigger girls going upwards, and the choir near the top. The Pinnacle was at the very top of the stairs as though her girls were a ladder leading to a high and holy place.

The hymn was 'Morning Has Broken'. Lyla loved that one and was wondering how one went about joining in when everyone else seemed to have a place to know what to do and where to be, when she spied Great Aunt Ada on the other side of the landing, also peering down over the balustrade. When Lyla joined her, Ada looked at her in a way that suggested she had just remembered Lyla's existence; that not only was she condemned to have a host of schoolgirls on her staircase at all hours, but on top of all that there was also another entirely separate girl who had somehow also come to be in her house.

'The world's adrift. No morning papers, no breakfast, and that infernal Pinsome on my stairs. It'll be howling and gongs and bells and what have you from day break to day end,' said Great Aunt Ada.

What was preoccupying Lyla, however, was her lack of uniform. She sighed and turned away from her aunt, wondering what to do with herself. And then it occurred to her that, since the Garden Hill girls might be kept on the stairs singing and praying for quite a while, it would be safe to sneak back into the North Gallery and have another look at the dorms. She could plan Escape Option Three after that, because on no account was she going to do any lessons with the Garden Hill Girls unless they were about something interesting.

As she entered the room, Lyla saw the sunlight on

the blue bedspreads and, as another hymn drifted up from below, she paused to savour the peace that comes with order and routine. She remembered her own unmade bed and thought too of Mop and how, at home in London, Mop's dresses would be draped about the place in artistic disorder.

Lyla tiptoed to the nearest wardrobe. Two grey dresses hung from the rail, two white shirts were folded on the shelf, and from the door hung a straw boater. She ran her fingers over the fabric of a school dress and down its pleated skirt. An unaccountable longing to see herself in it suddenly came over her. She glanced about, pulled Bucket from her sleeve and placed him on the bed. Swiftly she slipped the dress off the hanger and stepped into it, tugging it up over her yellow jersey. She looked at herself in the glass of the door, pulled her hair back and placed the hat on her head.

'Faye Peak won't be at all pleased if she sees you.'

Lyla jumped and reddened. A head appeared from between two beds: Catherine Lively – Cat – was there, and had been all along, huddled on the floor by the chimney, a book on her lap.

'Faye is in my year and she's the dorm prefect and she can be quite horrid . . . and she's always telling tales and sucking up to Mary Mary Unnecessary.'

Lyla's hands flew to the dress and fumbled at the fastening.

'I might tell Faye Peak What a Sneak that you tried on her dress,' said Cat.

Lyla reddened. Flustered and fumbling, she shook off the dress, letting it fall in a heap on the floor.

'Don't you go to school?'

'Mop – Mother says school makes you plain and clumpy.'

'Why actually are you here?'

'I'm not supposed to be here,' said Lyla.

'What do you mean?' asked Cat.

'I was stolen by Father and just abandoned here, so Mop is probably very worried and missing me very much.'

'Doesn't your mother know where you are?'

'No, and that's why I need to get back to her.' Lyla was enjoying having someone to talk to, so she added, 'Mop says life's unfair on women. And lots of people can be unkind because their feet are made of clay.'

'How can people's feet be made of clay?' asked Cat, frowning at all the turns and twists of Lyla's conversation.

'You're very literal-minded. If your feet are "made of clay", it actually means that your head has no poetry or romance in it. And people with feet of clay say unkind things.' As she spoke, Lyla thought about that, and her face darkened. She looked down and bit her lip.

'Do people say unkind things about your mother?' Cat asked.

'No, of course not,' answered Lyla very fast. 'But sometimes . . .' She paused, and Cat waited, but then Lyla picked up Bucket, stroked him and furled him about her shoulders because she didn't want to answer Cat's question.

'Who is that?' asked Cat, eyeing Bucket with curiosity.

'Oh, this is Bucket. He is a ferret and he's sleepy now because he's not very keen on mornings. He sleeps in a sock drawer and eats pillows.'

Cat giggled, then said, a little teasingly, 'I might also tell Faye Peak you put a *ferret* on her bed.'

Lyla was put out that Cat didn't seem at all jealous that she had her very own ferret when no one else did, but she was also wounded that Cat might think of telling tales on her to Faye Peak What a Sneak.

'I don't care what you tell *anyone* because I'm going home very soon,' snapped Lyla, and stomped out.

19

BREAKFAST

Ada, still on the Gallery, was wincing and grimacing at the clash of the breakfast crockery and cutlery below.

'Right then, young lady, you must join the girls, I suppose, since they are your guests.' Ada's eyes twinkled and she took Lyla's hand and led her firmly down the stairs towards the State Dining Room.

Lyla dragged her feet. 'I just wish I had a –' she tugged at her yellow jersey. 'It's just that everyone will stare at me.'

'Oh dear, you can't worry about that sort of thing, you know,' said Aunt Ada briskly.

'But they will,' whispered Lyla sullenly.

'Well, there's a war on, you know – we can't just get hold of dresses at the drop of a hat.' She saw Lyla's face and added encouragingly, 'Nevertheless, we'll see what we can do.'

Lyla saw that the State Dining Room was now filled with long, narrow tables and that behind each chair stood a girl, head dipped, hands clasped. A murmured *Amen* was followed by a terrific scraping of chairs.

Ada called out loudly, 'Solomon? Solomon!'

The girls fell silent and turned their heads towards them, and Lyla wished that her aunt were not wearing a canary and overalls.

'Ah, good morning, Pinwheel.'

'Pinnacle.'

'Yes, yes.'

Lyla, meanwhile, had seen Cat at a nearby table and ventured a smile, but Cat had turned her head aside. Thinking how much she'd like to have a friend like Cat, it occurred to Lyla that she could show Cat how sweet a ferret of your own could be and what fun it was to have one always about you, so she nudged Bucket.

Bucket stirred in her sleeve. A little black nose appeared at the hem of Lyla's cuff and twitched as it grew aware of the great quantity of scrambled powdered egg in the room. He slithered out in a great rush and state of nervous excitement and began to make loud *dook-dook-dook* noises – his tail vibrating and bushy – as he went off in search of powdered egg. But, once on the floor, Bucket discovered an alarming number of feet and chair legs, and his excitement turned to fear. He froze, arched his back and began a sort of war dance. Lyla tensed; things weren't going according to plan. But when she bent to fetch him, he made himself long and fast and disappeared under a table.

Then someone yelped and kicked out and Bucket sped about in frantic circles. There was a shriek, then another, and suddenly Cat had jumped up on to a chair and was hopping about and bending to nurse her ankle and Lyla saw that she'd been bitten and that Bucket had drawn blood.

Aunt Ada, divining the cause of the commotion, turned to Pinnacle and said smoothly, 'Pinprick, your girls are most disorderly.'

'Pinnacle.'

Cat glared at Lyla, and Lyla – a little upset about Bucket's wickedness and that he'd chosen Cat of all people to bite – went off in search of her ferret.

She found him trembling and hissing at the bottom of a log basket.

'That child must be reformed,' said Pinnacle.

'Oh no, that won't be necessary,' said Aunt Ada brightly. 'In my opinion, children are quite ruined by adults.'

Lyla unearthed Bucket and joined Ada, who wrapped an arm around her niece before turning to Pinnacle.

'You must tread lightly with the young, Pinsome. Very lightly.'

20

SIR WALTER RALEIGH'S DESK

'And what schools have you attended?'

Lyla, fascinated by all the changes that had come to pass in Sir Walter Raleigh's rooms since the Pinnacle had established herself in them, turned her head from the typewriter and the filing cabinets and then back to gaze across the worn leather desk top at the headmistress.

'Oh, I don't need to go to school at all. I have lessons at home.'

'I see. Well, what English have you done?'

'Oh, lots. I like English,' answered Lyla. 'But actually I've finished it.'

'*Finished* it?'

'Yes. Now I only need to read poetry and novels, because everything you ever need to know in life is in them.'

'Is that so? Grammar? Spelling? Are they in novels?'

Lyla nodded. *Of course they were.* Anyway, Garden Hill girls must be awfully stupid if they still needed to do spelling. Probably going to classes with them wouldn't be so bad after all because Lyla would be near the top of the class for spelling, so she answered confidently, 'Oh yes, I can spell all the things you need to spell. Even difficult words like *bombe glacée* and *syllabub*.'

'I see. And do your spelling classes take place at such places as the Connaught and Claridges?'

'Yes,' answered Lyla, her confidence growing as the Pinnacle placed a little cross on a sheet of paper. 'And any place that has menus. You see, Mop tests me in restaurants, to see if I am coming along all right.'

'I see . . . Comprehension?'

'Comprehension?' asked Lyla. 'I've never heard of needing to do that.'

The Pinnacle sighed. 'I see. And arithmetic – is that something you have heard of needing to do?'

'Oh yes, of course, but I don't need to do any more arithmetic at all, you see; I already know everything you need to know in that too. Winnie says I've got the knack of it and I don't need to do any more at all.' She paused and said proudly, 'I am quite good at arithmetic.'

'May I ask what topics you have actually covered?'

'Oh, arithmetic is always just adding. It's very dull really. Gas bill plus electricity bill plus coal plus carrots, potatoes, milk, and so on. All you do in arithmetic is add one thing to another – it's only addition, and never any subtraction.'

The Pinnacle paused and then said, 'I see. No algebra either, I take it, in the household budget?'

'Oh no – definitely not. You can go through a whole lifetime without ever finding algebra anywhere at all. It never comes in handy.'

The Pinnacle bent her head as she marked another cross further down her sheet, and Lyla eyed the tall edifice of her hair and wondered how many pins went into it to make it so high up.

'And your French. What level of French do you have?'

'Oh, my French is quite all right. Winnie doesn't know any French at all because she doesn't hold with foreign places, so French has to come out of menus. Mop says the Café de Paris has the best French in it, and even some operas are in French.' Lyla decided to expand on the matter of opera. 'I think French opera is just about all right, but French plays are awfully dull – Molière especially. Mop – Mother – says Molière is bad enough in English and no one should ever have to listen to him in French. She says he's *deadly*.'

The Pinnacle marked another cross further down her sheet of paper and looked over the tops of her glasses at Lyla. 'And who, may I ask, is Winnie?'

Lyla smiled to think of sweet Winnie who was so certain about everything and could reduce a bewildering and complex world to a set of aphorisms.

'She's my tutor. But she gets distracted easily from lessons – you know, if the bell rings. Because the bell is *always* ringing and people are *always* visiting or sending flowers and Mother is *always* needing cups of coffee or trays of drinks and Winnie has to press Mother's dresses and cook and scrub and pick things up off the floor and change the water in the cut flowers and—'

'I see.' The Pinnacle wrote down a hurried stream of angular letters and dots and dashes on her paper.

Lyla, growing uncomfortable, squinted at them, but they were as illegible as a doctor's prescription. She began to think that, actually, perhaps going to lessons wouldn't be so nice if you had to do things like arithmetic and algebra, so she said, 'Actually Mother doesn't believe in school.'

At this, the Pinnacle put down her pen and said a little wearily, 'Nevertheless, you do seem to have found yourself *in* one. Now, over there . . . We have collected some bits and pieces of uniform for you. Hand-me-downs, but that's the best we can do.'

Lyla's heart leaped. Everything would be all right with a uniform. She would be just like all the other girls, and no one would laugh at her. She rushed towards the pile of clothing on the windowsill as the Pinnacle added, 'And I will endeavour to do the best I can with you. *Under the circumstances*, that is. You will be in Miss Threadgold's class with Form IV. She

21

THE MUSIC ROOM

The shoes were at least a size too big. Lyla clodhopped along, trying to make them move at the same time as her feet and not get left behind. The dress was a little large too, but if she walked carefully the skirt swung and felt quite nice. The problem, however, was Bucket, who did not think highly of a prickly regulation school jersey. Nevertheless, all in all Lyla was feeling quite comfortable about just appearing at the door of a history class because of a) being in uniform, and b) the history class being a doddle probably because the Celts had never really done anything of interest at all, so it would all be over very soon.

'Lyla?' asked Miss Pigeon.

Lyla nodded.

'I should like you all to welcome Lyla Spence. Now, Lyla, over here, next to Faye. Faye will look after you.'

Faye Peak?

Lyla hunched her shoulders a little as she eyed Faye and wondered if Cat had said anything to her about trying on her clothes. Taking a seat, she looked surreptitiously about the room, eventually catching Cat's eye. Cat grinned and pointed at Lyla's dress and then at Faye and raised her eyebrows in amusement. Lyla bowed her head and glowered down at the exercise book on her desk.

Miss Pigeon had turned to the blackboard propped against the harpsichord.

'Lyla, can I assume you have some knowledge of the Celts?'

'They cut off their enemy's heads,' said Lyla promptly, 'and put them on the doors of their houses. I wouldn't do that . . . I mean, I wouldn't want heads on my house —'

'Good,' interrupted Miss Pigeon. 'That's enough, thank you, Lyla . . . Well, you will be able then to join the rest of the class in writing a thirty-minute essay on the diet, customs and houses of the Celts.'

'*Thirty minutes?*' asked Lyla.

She'd been once to the British Museum with Winnie. Winnie had found nothing of interest in any of the Ancient Britain section, and much to cause alarm in the Egyptian, and then she'd announced it was time to go home. 'Won't waste time on this lot either,' she'd remarked as she'd waddled back through the Iron and Bronze Ages, rummaging in her large black bag for a handkerchief and glancing sidelong at tiny, carefully preserved fragments of things. 'Not much to say for themselves, have they, this lot?'

Lyla picked up her pencil and began to write.

The Celts were here a very long time before anyone else, e.g. Jesus and the Romans, but the Celts never actually did anything except to discover iron, which had happened to be here all along so it shouldn't count as a discovery. I learned about the Celts in the British Museum. You can spend hours in the British Museum and not learn much about the Celts at all because it took them 750 years just to discover how to make weapons out of the iron that they found that was there anyway. They tattooed their bodies ALL OVER and wore their hair in spikes and put horns on their helmets and went into battle with no clothes on. I am not surprised they got overtaken because it's just silly to fight the Romans when you're totally naked except for the horns on your head.

Lyla raised her head to look about and saw that Faye was applying herself with great concentration to drawing a sort of anthill with grass on top of it. Lyla rolled her eyes and wondered who would ever bother to draw a house that was only made of mud and grass. She put down her pencil, determined not to waste any time on that sort of thing.

Now Faye was drawing something else, a hill

perhaps with lots of rings around it. Lyla rolled her eyes. A hill fort. Miss Pigeon would surely find that very boring, especially all the arrows and labels Faye was adding now. Lyla eyed Faye. Faye's hair was pretty and blonde, the ends of her plaits curling softly around her face.

'Have you finished, Lyla?' asked Miss Pigeon.

'Yes. It was quick and easy really because there's nothing interesting to know about the Celts, is there?'

'Well, Miss Spence, we are about to spend an entire term on the Celts and, furthermore, they happen to be my specialist subject,' snapped Miss Pigeon.

Lyla leaned back in her chair, open-mouthed and aghast. *A whole term on the Celts. How could that ever be necessary?*

'And what's more,' continued Miss Pigeon, 'I will not be spoken to like that. Put your hands on your head and remain that way until the rest of the class has finished writing.'

22

TO THE NORTH GALLERY

Lyla absolutely, definitely, needed to escape. She would certainly not spend a whole term sitting next to Faye Peak with her hands on her head learning about the Celts.

The problem was that Lyla had still not come up with another plan. She'd thought long and hard last night, and everything she'd come up with seemed likely to go wrong. Besides, it was hard to put your mind to anything when there were so many places you were supposed to be at particular times, and you were being given things called *tardies* for being late or some other thing, or for being naughty, even when *you* didn't think you'd done anything wrong at all.

The worst thing about everything was that because Cat still hadn't talked to her since being bitten by Bucket it was highly likely she'd tell Faye about Lyla going into her wardrobe. As she dressed, Lyla decided to see if Cat was skiving assembly so she could plead with her not to tell Faye anything. Once again, Lyla crept along to the North Gallery and down the centre of the room and did, in fact, find Cat there.

'Do you always skive assembly?'

'Haven't you gone back to London yet?' retorted Cat.

Lyla shook her head. 'Actually, I can't think of a new Escape Option just at the moment. Anyway, doesn't Pinnacle notice you're not at assembly?'

'Pinnacle is *transported* during prayer –' Cat gestured heavenwards with arms thrust wide – 'to HIGHER REALMS, so she doesn't notice such earthly things. Father says she was going to go to Oxford and then something happened that young ladies aren't supposed to do or know about and that's why she prays all the time.' Cat paused, and then said rather suddenly, 'Do you know *anything*? I mean, in lessons, you don't seem to know anything at all.'

'That's not true. I know lots of things – it's only that they're not quite the same things as you learn in school because most of them are pointless and, so far, I'm not actually impressed by school at all.'

The break bell went, and Cat sighed and rolled her eyes. 'We've got double geography now with Noddy – that's Miss Nodding.'

A stream of girls could be heard on the stairs.

'What will we learn in double geography?' asked Lyla, hoping for tiny islands and other interesting places and wondering if you learned about things that were more interesting than the Celts.

Cat turned to her with interest. 'Haven't you ever studied geography either?'

'No – you see, Winnie doesn't want to go anywhere further than Henley.'

'Winnie?'

'My governess. Well, she was *supposed* to be my governess, but she's been REQUISITIONED by Mop to do the house because there're so many things a woman has to do in a house, but one of Mop's rules is that if a man wouldn't do a thing, especially a thing about the house, then Mop mustn't do it either, and neither must I. That means Mop and I walk about past all the socks and things on floors as if we hadn't seen them because men never notice socks being left about on floors.'

Cat's mouth hung open, astonished, and Lyla, heartened by the impression she seemed to be making, continued.

'So Winnie has to do all the things men won't do, like picking up dirty socks.'

'Are there lots of socks in your house?' asked Cat, rather arch.

'That's a very *literal-minded* thing to ask,' said Lyla, equally arch.

Cat laughed. She shoved her book beneath a mattress, grabbed Lyla's hand and together they slipped out into the file of girls, and Lyla realized she still hadn't found out if Faye knew about her uniform or not.

Double geography was very disappointing, and after that came break-time, and once she'd stood in line for milk and biscuits Lyla saw that Miss Trumpet, who seemed to be in charge of mail, was standing beside Old Alfred and handing out letters, so she lingered nearby, hoping there'd be something from Mop. But Miss Trumpet got to the end of the Mail In tray and there was nothing for Lyla.

Everyone else was chatting in groups, and no one was including her in their group, so Lyla went to a corner of the hall, turned her back to the room, tore a sheet from her exercise book and sat down to write another letter to Mop.

> *Furlongs*
> *Ladywood*
> *North Devon*
>
> *Dearest Mop,*
>
> *The Pinnacle (she is the headmistress) is in Sir Walter Raleigh's Room, which is even bigger than Aunt Ada's, but she needs a big room because she has all the company of heaven with her and that needs spacious accommodation. Solomon is very protective of*

Furlongs and very concerned about the Laundry being used for domestic science classes, the Orangery for art classes, the Music Room for French and history, as well as upset that all the corridors smell of cauliflower.

Faye laughs when she sees me because I clop around a bit in my shoes as they are too big. When Faye laughs, everyone else laughs too, because everyone wants to be friends with Faye.

We did games yesterday. Pigeon teaches games and history but she is even worse at games than she is at history because of her head going in and out when she walks. That is what happens to you if you have a surname like Pigeon, but if you giggle at her she threatens you with Black Jake. Black Jake is actually only an outdoor plimsoll.

By the way, Garden Hill girls do algebra, but I told the Pinnacle you can get along quite well without algebra because you don't ever use it in your whole life, so maybe I won't have to do it. I did double geography, but it was no good because there were only estuaries in it and I can't see why they're interesting at all.

Do you ever worry about me? I know worrying can make you ill and I know I should just flick worries away, sort of like flicking a fly from my shoulder. I do try to do that but they just come back again.

One worry that won't go away is that I almost made a friend. She is called Cat, but she doesn't like me any more, all because of Bucket. The other girls who are my age who I know so far are:

1. Edith, who is wet and weedy.
2. Flea (actually Felicita), who faints on purpose to get out of playing a thing called lacrosse, which happens to be the silliest game ever invented.
3. Brenda, who never has anyone to talk to.
4. Elspeth, who is even worse than me at everything and always moaning about her chillblains.
5. Faye Peak, who sucks up to everyone especially the head girl. Faye is dorm prefect and I don't like her.
6. Imelda, who you wouldn't like because her feet are made of clay.
7. Mary Masters who is the head girl and she is horrid but not as horrid as Faye.

I have to eat lunch and tea with the Lower School in the Red Library. Now Prudence has to make school things like sago and semolina and they taste horrid because Prudence is NO GOOD AT PUDDINGS and because she has no one to help her because she won't allow the school staff into her kitchens.

No one talks to me and they all stare and I am really very unhappy, and they all whisper about me and laugh at me behind my back. The only person who likes me is Bucket. I gave him a ping-pong ball and he was very delighted about that.

Every day Imelda says there will be bombs in London any minute now, and I do so hope you will write and tell me that everything is all right, because it's very hard to be worried about your mother all day. Have we been bombed? Is home still there?

Every day I hope there'll be a letter, but there never is, so please, please write.

Lyla decided not to say anything about putting her hands on her head in history as she wasn't sure at all what Mop would think about that and wrote instead:

Don't worry because soon I will get a new plan and it won't go wrong and soon I will come home.

All my love,

Lyla

23

THE ANCIENT GREEKS

Art had looked as if it might be fun because the teacher, Miss Primrose, might actually have been born in the current century and was really quite young and pretty. Not as pretty as Mop, Lyla decided, but still. She expected that art would be even easier than history because she was quite good at drawing, even if doing it with a Ferret up your sleeve was a bit tricky.

Another thing that was nice was that Cat had chosen the easel next to Lyla, and all was going well until the Pinnacle appeared at the door. She paused there and surveyed the Orangery. Her eyes focused on the statues that lined the room, which were perhaps plundered from an acropolis or other ancient place. Pinnacle's lips tightened.

'Put down your charcoal immediately. This will not do; it is most improper. Your scarves girls, quickly, around the lower parts of those statues. They must be covered.'

Lyla's hand-me-downs had not included a scarf, but

when the rest of the class returned from the makeshift cloakroom in the lobby of the Orangery, she helped Cat tie hers around the lower parts of Odysseus, and as they did so they caught each other's eyes and both giggled.

'Lyla Spence, you would do a great deal better at this school if you were to behave a little less like a small child,' said Pinnacle.

Lyla's cheeks burned. She hurried back to her easel and lowered her head.

Pinnacle continued to watch Lyla intently. 'It is high time that you grew up.'

'Nonsense, Pintuck.' Great Aunt Ada had drifted into the Orangery. 'The problem with the world –' she took Pinnacle by the elbow – 'is that there are *too many* grown-ups in it, don't you think?' Ada released her grip and looked around, her gaze alighting on the Ancient Greeks, and with a twinkle of amusement she said. 'My word! What on earth has happened to my marbles? Do my Romans and Greeks have a chill? Marvellous, Pinfish, marvellous, very fetching. I wonder Phidias never thought of *scarves*.'

That night, still stinging from Pinnacle's instruction to *grow up*, Lyla paced about her room and eventually decided that she must write to Mop once more, because there were some things she needed to know and she had no one else to ask.

Furlongs
Ladywood
North Devon

Dearest Mop,

*People are always telling me to grow up and maybe
I <u>am</u> growing up more slowly than other people –
but most of the time I actually feel already all
grown up on the inside so perhaps its only on the
outside that I look young. Great Aunt Ada makes
me feel like that because somehow she's got all
inside out, all young on the inside but crumpled on
the outside.*

*Anyway, I don't know how to grow up any quicker.
I do lots of grown-up things with you, but perhaps
doing grown-up things isn't the same as being
grown up. Anyway, I don't think you <u>can</u> rush
growing up. It takes longer than people say. That's
true, isn't it?*

*I so wish you were here to tell me that and lots of
other things that one needs to know. How to make
friends, for example. Everyone else knows how to
do that but I don't, and they don't teach you any
of those useful sorts of things in schools – they only
teach you about dim people like Celts; that's how I*

know you're right about there being no need
for school.

All my love,

Lyla

24

THE MAIL IN TRAY

It was break-time again, and once again Lyla went to join the group around Miss Trumpet. Poor Old Alfred was a little overshadowed now by the great pile of mail that seemed to arrive every day in the Mail In tray, but somehow Lyla still seemed to feel his steely gaze on her as she waited. The pile was diminishing, and Lyla began to tense. *Surely Mop would have written by now.* Cat had a letter from her parents and so did Mary Masters. It was normal for parents to write.

'*Elspeth Gibbs, Elsie Flynn, Liza Durham . . .*'

Miss Trumpet rattled off names – every name, it seemed, but that of Lyla Spence.

'*Lyla Spence.*'

Lyla spun round and leaped towards Miss Trumpet, almost snatching it from her hands. Only then her hand hesitated over the envelope. She froze for a second, then raised her chin a little and stepped back.

'Actually, I don't want it.'

'And what am I to do with it?'

'Well, you see, I don't read letters from my father. The letters that come from Father have to be given to Solomon,' said Lyla. 'He makes them into fighter planes and sends them off.' She made a meandering gesture with her arm, then turned her back and stalked out as everyone stared after her.

25

A VICKERS WELLINGTON
LN514 IN THE DAMSON

My darling Lyla,

Things are not going well for us in France. The troops in the north east are surrounded and we are forced to retreat and must somehow hope to get the rest of our men safely home, but it will be a race against time.

Thank heavens Churchill is at last in power. Thank heavens too for South Africa and Canada who have come in on our side. Things may well, one day, take a turn for the better.

Enough of this. I imagine that at Furlongs the war will seem very far away to you, but perhaps you will think sometimes of me, and perhaps one day you will think more kindly of me too.

You will always be everything to me.

Yours always,

Father

26

THE QUEEN'S HORSES

Lyla heard a knock. Cautiously she opened the door, and there was Cat, facing Lyla through the half-open door. Cat paused, then asked, 'Why won't you read letters from your father?' asked Cat.

'Did Trumpet give the letter to Solomon?' demanded Lyla.

'Yes, but why did she have to give it to him?' asked Cat.

'Because he has a gift for fighter planes, and fighter planes are what you turn letters into if you don't want them,' answered Lyla.

'That's not at all normal,' said Cat.

'I don't care if you don't think I'm normal,' responded Lyla.

'Not just not normal, Lyla – *peculiar*. That's what you are.'

'Certain things have made me that way,' replied Lyla. 'Things and *people*,' she added darkly, turning away. 'Anyway, I don't care if everyone stares and talks about me behind my back.' She whirled back round to face Cat. '*You* wouldn't read his letters either if he was *your* father.' She paused and saw that she had Cat's full attention, and because she so rarely had anyone's full attention, she continued, 'He *left* us. That's why I don't read his letters. He left us, then he stole me and dumped me here.'

'Stole you?' said Cat, walking to the bed and sitting on the edge of it.

Lyla was pleased Cat had done that, so she went over and sat by her.

'Yes, you see, Mop – Mother – doesn't know where I am. She isn't answering my letters and that might be because someone is taking them or the post is losing them, because none of them arrive, and so that's why I have to actually go to her in London and it's very, very urgent because I'm worried about her.'

'I see. Well, you could go by train?' suggested Cat.

'I did try to go by train,' snapped Lyla, 'but the trains don't stop here unless Great Aunt Ada tells them to. And there's no getting through to Great Aunt Ada because she eats dinner with her horse, keeps dead armadillos in her hall and knights in her corridors and goes about with a pistol in her pocket and a canary on her shoulder, and because she has a butler who puts his head in the jaws of Asiatic lions . . . so you see, nothing here is *normal* –'

Cat, bemused, hesitated. Then, presumably

deciding *one thing at a time*, asked, 'Does she really eat dinner with her horse?'

'Yes, Violet eats Welsh rarebit every night off a silver salver that comes up in a dumb waiter.'

Cat looked bewildered, so Lyla thought perhaps she should elaborate.

'Yes, every night at seven. And that is one of the many symptoms of her dottiness and why she doesn't understand at all how urgent it is I go home.'

'But why don't you just tell your father to take you home?' asked Cat.

'Of course I can't, because he's the person who *put* me here in the first place,' snapped Lyla. 'You can't ask for help from people who leave you and then steal you and put you somewhere you're not supposed to be without ever asking your feelings on the matter. Besides, he's at war.'

Cat nodded slowly. Then, as if for inspiration, gazed about at the hares and the unicorns on Lyla's walls, and after a while said, 'I think I've got an idea . . . You have to hide someone or something from your great aunt that she loves very much so she knows what it feels like not to have it. Then, when she's upset, you do a trade. She has her thing back and you go back to your mother.'

That was actually quite a good idea, but in fact Lyla was disappointed Cat should be so willing to help her leave, because if Cat were her friend she would surely want Lyla to stay. So instead she just answered quietly, 'I'll have a think.'

However, having thought about the matter, Lyla couldn't think of any person that fitted the bill, because it was too dangerous to lock a lion tamer up and too cruel to lock Prudence up. So eventually she reached a decision.

'Violet. It'll have to be Violet.'

Cat grinned. 'The horse?' She giggled, then jumped up, reeling with laughter so that Lyla wasn't sure she was entirely serious when she said, 'Come on, let's look for somewhere to put her.'

They decided in the end on the Maharajah's Room because it was unoccupied and near to Lyla's and because, anyway, Aunt Ada would never know where Violet was because in a house like Furlongs you could live in the West Wing and have no idea that the whole Household Cavalry was in any other wing.

'Is it actually possible to make a horse climb a flight of stairs?' asked Cat.

'Oh yes,' answered Lyla, who wasn't in fact sure at all. 'The Queen's horses go up stairs all the time.'

'Do they?'

Lyla nodded.

'I don't believe you'd really do it,' said Cat, eyes sparkling.

Because Lyla wanted Cat to admire and like her,

she answered, 'Of course I would.'

Delighted by the absurdity of the notion, Cat took Lyla's hand and whispered, 'You'll have to wait till tomorrow. After lunch it's gymnastics and we're going to do that in the Undercroft, and that's good for two reasons. First, you can't hear anything down there; and second, it's really easy to skive gymnastics because Pigeon doesn't notice anything.'

27

THE MAHARAJAH'S ROOM

Lyla entered the State Dining Room at lunch the following day hoping to sit next to Cat, but because she was late as usual there was only one place left in the room and that was opposite Faye Peak. Lyla slowly walked over to it and reluctantly pulled out the chair. As she sat, Faye pulled a face. Lyla glanced around the room, wondering where Cat was.

No one at her table said hello or smiled at Lyla and she couldn't see Cat, so she looked down at her plate. There was an uncomfortable silence. Sitting opposite Faye made Lyla feel guilty about going into her wardrobe. She glanced up at her and felt annoyed that Faye's hair was so tidy and blonde and that she did everything perfectly, even drawing perfect Celtic round houses just because Pigeon wanted her to.

Slowly the rest of the table resumed their talk, but it was only among themselves, and Lyla, not for the first time, had the sensation that her loneliness was a thing made visible by the space and the silence around her, the bubble of emptiness that went wherever she went.

After a while she shrugged and made a conscious effort to turn her thoughts to *the matter in hand*: the task of getting an elderly horse up a large set of stairs.

She ate her chicken but pushed the carrots carefully to one side. She wasn't entirely sure that horses ate boiled carrots, but she brushed that concern away because now there was something else on her mind, and that was Bucket.

Bucket was in fact very clever about things like school timetables and always started to get wriggly at meal times, and now because of the proximity of chicken he was doubly excitable and trying to turn around inside her sleeve. Lyla sighed; it was so difficult trying to be just like everyone else if you were the only person with a restless and greedy ferret trying to do a U-turn in your sleeve. When apples were handed round, Lyla peeled her one, cut it into eight precise segments and then slipped them along with the carrots into her pocket.

'Gross,' said Faye. 'Did you see what she did?'

Faye wrinkled her face so much that she suddenly became rather plain, and Lyla wondered if she ought to tell her about getting lines because Mop said you got wrinkles from grimacing, and if Faye could wrinkle her nose about just a small thing like boiled carrots being in pockets she'd be as lined as a crossword puzzle before she was twenty.

Bucket began to hiss and Lyla tried to shush him.

'Ughhh!' screeched Faye, struggling frantically to extricate herself from the bench and the table. 'She's got that *thing* with her.'

Then suddenly everyone around Lyla was standing up and scraping their chairs, moving hurriedly to join Faye at the door, all looking disgusted.

Left alone at the table, Lyla scowled.

She didn't care if Faye became a crossword puzzle when she was twenty and she didn't care what Faye thought about soggy carrots in pockets or about ferrets at meal tables, because she, Lyla, would soon be leaving. Nevertheless, Lyla's eyes were brimming and she bent her head to hide them.

'Hello.' It was Cat. She'd seen Lyla was alone and she'd come over from wherever she'd been just to sit with her.

Lyla raised her eyes.

'Faye Peak What a Sneak?' asked Cat.

Lyla nodded.

'Take no notice of her. Anyway, Faye would never be brave enough to take a horse upstairs.' Cat squeezed Lyla's hand.

Lyla looked up at her, grateful but uncertain whether she herself would indeed be brave enough when it came to actually taking Violet upstairs.

'Come on,' said Cat.

Lyla, with the soggy carrots and the apple in her

pocket and Bucket up her sleeve, stood up, smiled at Cat and together they left the room.

'Good luck,' said Cat.

Lyla eventually found Violet wandering loose on the old grass tennis court. Lyla called to her and, because Violet had never known any unkindness, she padded trustingly towards her. Lyla opened the gate and patted her pocket to tell her there were interesting things in it, and Violet bent her head and nuzzled Lyla's skirt.

So far, so good, thought Lyla. She led Violet along the path between the yew hedges, eyeing the door ahead with some trepidation. It was low and, for so grand a house, narrow. *First the door,* she told herself, *then the stairs. The stairs will be the trickiest, so I must keep the apple in reserve.*

Violet, a fine-boned and delicate horse, made her way through the doorway as though she were entirely accustomed to entering ancient stone houses. Everything was quiet. The girls were all in the Undercroft with Pigeon; the staff still probably lunching in the Housemaids' Parlour; Ada and Solomon probably in the Billiard Room. Stretching her neck towards Lyla's pocket, she trotted across the hall, picking her way around the wingback chairs and occasional tables.

At the foot of the stairs, Lyla, remembering how

Cat trusted her to be brave enough to do this, stood on tiptoe and whispered, 'Do this for me, Violet, *please*.'

Lyla stepped on to the first tread and tugged gently at Violet's mane, and was already thinking of how, later on, she would be telling Cat all about it . . . but Violet hesitated.

'Come *on*,' hissed Lyla, holding out some apple and putting her left foot on to the second step. Violet pawed the stair and snorted, then pawed it again. Lyla went up higher, holding the hand with the apple just out of Violet's reach. Violet placed a hoof on the first step.

'It means I can go home,' begged Lyla.

Violet stretched to the apple and snorted with frustration to find that it should still be beyond reach. Lyla had begun to think of all the Form IV girls doing gym in the Undercroft while she, Lyla Spence, happened for some reason to be trying to coax an elderly mare up a flight of cantilevered stairs, when suddenly Violet lunged forward. There was an unnerving skidding as she placed first one foreleg then the other on the stairs. Lyla, trembling, held out her hand, and Violet, despite the inconvenience of being half up and half down, chomped the apple. Fumbling about for more apple, Lyla stepped backwards. With a terrific clattering, finally both of Violet's forelegs were on the tread and she reached the apple and munched noisily.

Lyla took another slice of apple from her pocket as she stepped backwards up another step, and whispered in a shaky voice, 'Yes, good girl, come on – we've got to be quick.' It was frightening to have a horse partway up a staircase. Violet's rear-right hoof lifted and searched clumsily for the tread. She snorted and pawed at the stairs, and Lyla, unnerved, stepped back up again, and at that very moment Violet suddenly got the idea into her head that it was easier to take staircases all in one go, and she lurched and staggered and lunged all the way to the top making a frightful racket, legs all at awkward angles, clumsy and clattering. Lyla, terrified, raced full tilt upwards, keeping just ahead of Violet.

Now Violet was on level ground, she trotted determinedly after Lyla and the apple, while Lyla backed hurriedly down the corridor, the apple in her outstretched hand. 'Not so fast, yes, yes, in here,' she whispered urgently. Lyla backed into the Maharajah's Room, and Violet followed. Shutting the door firmly behind them, Lyla collapsed flat against it, puffing and panting.

'Phew. Well done, clever girl,' she whispered. 'Now you can have all the apple you want.' She emptied her pockets on to the crewel-work bedspread, and Violet nudged and calmly sorted out the best pieces as though all her life she'd eaten sliced apple from a maharajah's bed. 'Aunt Ada has twenty-eight bedrooms, so when she notices you're gone, it'll take her *forever* to find you.'

She opened the windows for Violet, then left, closing the door behind her, turning the lock and pocketing the key, rather pleased because now she could go and tell Cat that Violet was installed in the Maharajah's Room.

28

REAR-END BUCKETS

Lyla was supposed to be doing Prep in the Red Library, but since she had no intention of drawing diagrams of Celtic hill forts, she decided instead to wander about and see if Great Aunt Ada had noticed that Violet was missing.

She spied Ada in the knot garden, an embattled, faded sort of hat on her head, a basket over her arm. She was taking cuttings in a scientific kind of way from the roses, and making precise notes in a mildewed logbook. Lyla watched, very tempted to mention Violet's name in a casual, offhand kind of way just to see if Great Aunt Ada had noticed that her horse was missing. Then, growing hungry, she began to wonder if it was nearly dinner and almost Welsh Rarebit o'clock.

The gong sounded from the hall. Ada raised her eyes to the courtyard clock, saw that it was indeed seven, and, with a sigh of satisfaction, set down her basket. The last echo of the gong died and, at that point, Lyla heard a whinny that issued from a first-floor window.

Ada looked about distractedly. Lyla, panic-stricken, crept behind the potting shed. Violet whinnied again, and Lyla could see her nostrils flaring, and her eyes wide in astonishment – that she should find herself so far above the grass. Lyla flapped her arms about as if that might quiet her, but Violet whinnied once more, at which point Ada looked upwards and saw the horse peering in an interested, intelligent sort of way out of the maharajah's window – alarmed, it seemed, that the trees should be below her.

Everything had gone wrong. Now Ada knew exactly where her horse was and she'd never fulfil her part of the deal.

Lyla eyed her great aunt and saw that a tender, motherly smile had formed on her lips, as though Violet were a charming and mischievous child.

'Ah, Violet,' Ada hollered up, 'there you are.' At the sound of her mistress's voice, Violet's ears twitched, and she quietened and turned her head in the direction of Ada, who continued, 'Good, good, very sensible, yes, the Maharajah's Room is as safe a place as any to spend a war. Most resourceful of you, Violet – I do wonder you thought of that all on your own. Resourceful. Accomplished. Daring. Determined.'

As Lyla wondered if Great Aunt Ada were entirely

serious in thus addressing her horse it came to Violet's attention that the top of a rowan tree came conveniently up to the first floor, and she nuzzled it and began to eat the soft tips of it.

'Very good, Violet, very good. Marvellous, marvellous. I shall send you up a climbing rose. A Rambling Rector perhaps, a hydrangea and a clematis – yes, a vigorous clematis. You should like that, shouldn't you? – yes, a clematis will romp up there in a week or two.' Aunt Ada chuckled merrily, then, turning to look about, she located Lyla and fixed those laughing, gold-flecked sorcerer eyes upon her.

'She'll have to take her morning exercise in the ballroom, you know, and up and down the corridors . . . I am not sure you ever took Violet's happiness into consideration, did you? You will find life easier if you don't think only of yourself, you know.'

'I don't think only of myself,' said Lyla sullenly. 'I think of Mop. That's who I think of. All the time.'

Lyla was stung at the injustice of Ada's comment, so she began to slink and creep away from her towards the house, cross that *everything had gone wrong. AGAIN.*

She stomped into the State Dining Room, chose a chair in the furthest corner, scraped it into position and sat there with hunched shoulders. The rest of the girls began to file in after her and take their places. Finally Cat entered the room and saw Lyla. She rushed over and pulled out the chair next to her.

'Did you do it?' Cat whispered.

'I did, but it all went wrong.'

'Violet is upstairs? Actually upstairs?' whispered Cat.

Lyla nodded and glared into the thick skin that lay, as usual, across the surface of Prudence's pink blancmange.

'Great Aunt Ada knows, and she just thinks it's funny and doesn't mind at all, and Violet doesn't mind because there's a tree to eat outside the window, so it was all for nothing.'

Cat grinned, delighted by the whole adventure, but Lyla was still cross that it had all been in vain, so she put down her spoon and was about to leave when Great Aunt Ada steamed in. Lyla sat down again very quickly.

Heads turned, but Great Aunt Ada smiled and announced breezily to all the room, 'Violet'll need hay, of course. In the maharajah's bedroom at 8 a.m. and 4 p.m., please.' Her eyes found Lyla, and she continued sweetly. 'Lyla, she'll need a bucket too, for her rear end. Three times a day for the rear-end bucket down; twice a day for the front-end bucket up.'

Lyla's cheeks reddened and she scowled into her blancmange.

Rear-end buckets down? Hay up? Up and down all those stairs so many times a day?

Cat giggled, so Lyla scowled at her too and hissed, 'Well, it was your idea.'

The Pinnacle appeared from the opposite door and the two women faced each other across the room, like opposing armies, the light of battle in their eyes.

'Am I right in thinking that there's a *horse* in the house? I was never given to understand there'd be a *horse* on the premises.'

'My dear Pinhead,' answered Aunt Ada, 'this is my house, and my horse, and I shall put them just wherever I want them.'

'Pinnacle.'

'Of course, Pinnacle, *quite* – but, as I say, this being *my* house and Violet being *my* horse, I'll do as I like with them both.' With that, Ada sailed out of the room.

Lyla, with a hurried scraping of her chair, rose and pushed her way across the room and ran down the corridor after her aunt. She caught her up outside the Billiard Room.

'I could always bring Violet down again?' she volunteered.

'Out of the question. She'll *never* make it down again, d'you see? It's the way their hips and knees are made – they don't like *down* because they can't see where they're putting their feet – horses do very much like to see where they're putting their feet.'

'*Never?*' asked Lyla, such an eventuality not having

occurred to her. She stalled, until with a flash of inspiration, she said, 'I know. We can build a ramp.'

'You may have noticed,' said Aunt Ada, peering dimly down at Lyla, 'that in a war there tends to be a great shortage of men about the place to build ramps for horses that find themselves upstairs. Besides, I intend to give Violet the full run of the place. I should like her to come and greet me of a morning, and we could turn the ballroom over to lawn, there's plenty of rot and damp in that sprung maple floor and – you never know – horses may not actually be at all averse to oriental luxury in their sleeping quarters, silk rugs and so forth. Not to mention the luxuriant new growth of my favourite rowan tree.'

Without another word, Great Aunt Ada turned on her heel and marched away.

29

TOOTH-BRUSHING

A shrill whinny reverberated down the corridor. Violet was ready to make her morning visit to Great Aunt Ada's room.

Lyla glared at the unicorns and at the white hares and then at the writing table and then at everything else, furious with everything. *Now there was Violet as well as Mop to worry about.*

Violet began to clip-clop about in the excitable manner that announced she would like her door to be opened. Lyla, thinking of the silky floor coverings that maharajahs liked to walk over barefoot, grabbed her toothbrush and went to keep Violet company, but Violet only turned and flicked her tail and trotted to the window.

They stood together at the open window, Violet first sniffing the dew then nuzzling the climbing hydrangea and plucking off its lace-cap flowers and swishing her tail and appearing very pleased that a delicious plant had come all the way up to a first-floor window. Lyla brushed her teeth. Tooth-brushing was, in fact, less boring in the company of a horse.

Next, Lyla took an ivory-backed hairbrush from the washstand and began to groom Violet's coat. Tending to a horse was altogether a less alarming affair than worrying about Mop. She stood on tiptoe and told Violet, 'I'll write to Mop today because my letters are getting lost in the post, or perhaps Winnie is forgetting to pass them on. You see, Violet, letters are a bit like prayers, quite haphazard really – you can't be sure they'll *actually* arrive.'

'You see, I told you she'd done it.'

Lyla froze at the voice and turned crimson. She'd been caught red-handed talking to a horse. She turned to see Cat and Imelda in the doorway.

'Actually, I *have* to talk to Violet because she can't go downstairs because horses have the wrong kind of knees,' Lyla snapped.

Cat grinned with amusement at the sight of a horse amidst oriental rugs and silk hangings. Imelda stared open-mouthed and then ran off, probably to tell everybody about Violet but Cat lingered at the door.

'I'm still so impressed you did it, you know.'

'But it didn't work,' said Lyla.

Cat paused, then said, 'I talked to Solomon, you know, about your letters from your father. He's very sad about you not reading them, and I am too.'

With that, Cat turned and ran off down the hallway.

Lyla bowed her head. She wanted a letter from *Mop*. That was what she wanted more than anything else. She ran her fingers over Violet's soft muzzle and whispered, 'She doesn't understand what it's like to be me. No one understands what it's like to be me.'

She decided to head back to her room, for it was time to write another letter to Mop.

Furlongs
Ladywood
Devon

Dearest Mop,

You have to have so many different bits of uniform –
Summer Knickers and Winter Knickers and even
Outer Knickers, which are for gymnastics. Because of
the uniform I suppose I LOOK quite like everybody
else, but still I don't FEEL like everybody else.

The bad thing about my uniform is that it is all
only hand-me-downs from a fifth-former called Jo
Wicker who left. Faye thinks it's funny I have to
wear Wicker's uniform, because Wicker was the most
unpopular girl in her year. Faye gets lots of letters
from her family, but everyone likes her because she's

pretty and does whatever the teachers say.

Miss Threadgold is the maths teacher and the form teacher, but they call her Threadlegs because she looks like she's made of pipe cleaners. She is always telling me off for being late. ALSO, she made Bucket wait outside double maths because she found Bucket inside her handbag and that upset her a great deal because she thinks ferrets are dirty and unpredictable, unlike numbers, which behave in a clean and predictable way.

Art is with Miss Primrose and we draw on brown wrapping paper because you can't get any white paper any more. You would like Primrose. She reads poetry while we draw because poetry stops your head getting in the way of your heart and that's important because feeling in drawing is more important than accuracy. Imelda says Primrose is FAST. You can tell that because she cuts her hair short and in a straight line like a lampshade. I know that's not true because your hair is short and quite like a lampshade too, but I didn't tell Imelda that.

Also, Great Aunt Ada doesn't have enough bathrooms or hot water so we have to queue and share our baths and are only allowed SIX inches of water, and Miss Macnair the Matron is very fierce about that, and even G. A. Ada has the six-inch line on her bath. If you fill it up more, someone is sure to tell on you, especially someone like Brenda. Brenda is always on her own because she doesn't have any friends. She doesn't have a mother, only a father, and he is in the Far East. Sometimes I feel sorry for Brenda, but I don't really like her.

Imelda is always pretending to be sick so she can lie about in the San, because the San has its own fire and its own bath and you can have as much hot water in it as you like. Tomorrow I am going to give Bucket a new ball of string as he hid the last one in a laundry basket and it got ruined in the wash. Also Aunt Ada says she is going to give me some writing paper to write to you because I am running out, but paper is very hard to get in a war.

Are you doing war work, like knitting? Lots of Garden Hill Mothers do that AND they write lots of letters and everyone reads their letters to each other at break-time. Every day I wait for a letter from you and it never comes.

Oh, Mop, I am no good at anything because of being taught by Winnie. Winnie doesn't know any of the things you learn in school. I have done everything I can to get home, but nothing works out and it just goes wrong all the time, and now Violet is stuck upstairs in an Indian bedroom and everyone sees me with her rear-end buckets and stares at me so *PLEASE DON'T LEAVE ME HERE*. I don't know how to make friends so I only have Bucket to talk to mostly. Cat tries to talk to me, but she asks so many questions and I find them difficult to answer.

Please don't forget my birthday, because everyone gets presents on their birthdays, and please, please write because it makes me sad and scared when you don't and maybe one day I will be too sad to ever write to you again.

All my love,

Lyla

30

LETTERS AND NUMBERS MIXED

'Late, Lyla Spence.' Threadgold put a tardy next to Lyla's name. Lyla had already collected several tardies for not being in the right place at the right time as well as a SCEL for bringing a horse into the house. A SCEL was a very alarming thing, short for 'sceler', which was a word for wicked in an ancient language and meant you got a big black mark by your name on the noticeboard.

'Sit there, please, next to Imelda.'

Imelda rolled her eyes and turned aside. Imelda did whatever Faye did – that was why she'd rolled her eyes. Lyla sat down. Faye just wanted to be like Mary Masters; she wanted to be head of the school one day and carry Pinnacle's books around. Still, it was annoying the way that everyone copied whatever Faye said and did.

Threadgold went from desk to desk. She was very ancient, and when she moved about she made a rustling sound like dry leaves. She always wore the same suit and the same lace-up shoes with socks, and always left the scent of talcum powder behind her wherever she went.

'Turn over. You have thirty minutes.'

Lyla lifted her chin and walked quickly between the desks to the back next to Imelda, as instructed. She hadn't known there'd be *exams*. She gazed at her sheet, bewildered. The only kind of mathematics Winnie knew about didn't have any letters and brackets. Anyway, she'd never done any kind of exam. She scowled at the formulae on the sheet of paper and then around the class and saw lots of pencils moving earnestly and swiftly across sheets.

After a while she put her hand up because she could make no sense of anything and thirty minutes was feeling like a very long time.

'Put your hand down, Lyla Spence. No doubt you haven't covered this topic?'

Lyla gazed at the bookshelves and at the oil paintings and wondered if any of the people in the portraits had done sums with letters and numbers mixed up. Then she looked at the clock and then around the room again and at the back of Cat's head, because Cat was just in front of her, and then at Imelda, who had almost finished her sheet. Imelda glared at Lyla and turned her sheet face down in a huffy sort of way, but Lyla noticed that Cat had moved her sheet and all the answers on it were clear and legible, so she grabbed her pencil and began to write.

31

COVENTRY

Hearing a feverish whispering emanating from the hall, Lyla paused to watch, and saw that the girls were huddled in close-knit clusters, then separating and re-forming in new clusters, like a kaleidoscopic pattern, only from time to time one girl would detach herself and go to the noticeboard and quickly return, pointing and beckoning.

Lyla's pulse began to race and her heart to pound – the results of the mathematics exam was on that board for all to see. She headed down the stairs, chin tilted, arms swinging defiantly to show she didn't care. Nevertheless, as the hall grew silent and heads turned, heat and colour rose to her cheeks.

Pinnacle saw Lyla and paused. Then she took up the school bell and began brusquely cutting a swathe through the girls, scattering them with sweeping arabesques of her arm and a violent ringing of the bell.

Lyla, eyes fixed on the noticeboard, made her way

towards it, trying very much to look as though she didn't care that girls pulled aside when she passed. She stared at the board. The name of every single girl was listed in year groups, and beside every name was a percentage mark in black. Only by Lyla's name there was a *red* mark and the word 'DISQUALIFIED'.

Disqualified.

The whole school could see that Lyla Spence of Year Two was DISQUALIFIED.

'Cheating, Lyla Spence. Garden Hill girls do not cheat.' The Pinnacle gripped Lyla's arm and propelled her along the great length of the North Corridor.

Ahead of them Great Aunt Ada, singing loudly to herself, emerged abruptly from the Billiard Room and blew towards them like a spring squall. Pinnacle tightened her grip and quickened her pace, determined to ignore the mistress of the house, but Ada barred her way and said breezily, 'Ah, good morning, Pinion.'

Under her arm was an item Lyla had never seen attached to the person of her great aunt before: a large rolled paper. Lyla eyed it, fearful of what Ada might do, for there was a sprightly, wicked air about her today.

'And tell me, Pinfish, have your girls taught you anything yet this morning? They're the best teachers, the young, are they not? Remarkable for their ardour and curiosity, for the clarity with which they see things, is that not so? We must try every day to be more like a child, to remember what it was to be a child. They should be in charge, yes, of course, I quite agree, the staff must be assessed by the pupils, not the other way round at all.' Aunt Ada swept onwards, murmuring to herself, 'Yes, it's all quite topsy-turvy as it is.'

Pinnacle pushed Lyla through the door into the French class. 'Catherine Lively, Lyla Spence,' she announced, 'you two will see me at 5 p.m. today for detention. The rest of you are to understand that these girls are in Coventry for the week – do you understand, Form IV?'

Lyla, who didn't know what Coventry was, glanced sidelong at Cat as she passed, but Cat hunched her shoulders and turned, and when Lyla sat at her desk and opened her French exercise book she found a note.

DON'T EVER COPY MY WORK AGAIN
OR TRY TO TALK TO ME.
I AM NOT YOUR FRIEND ANY MORE.

Lyla looked up and smiled. She'd never had a friend before. Cat might not be her friend *now*, but now at least Lyla knew that she had once had a friend, and that friend was Cat: the person she most liked.

32

THE UNDERCROFT

Lyla and Cat sat at opposite ends of the arctic, crypt-like place known as the Undercroft. Pinnacle sat between them, invigilating detention, which in this case was to memorize the books of the New Testament and write them out a hundred times. From time to time Pinnacle would summon them to recite the names of the books and, if they faltered, would dismiss them to resume the copying out once more.

Pinnacle went to the door to answer a query from Primrose, and Lyla took her opportunity to speak.

'I thought you put your paper there *especially* so I could see it,' she whispered.

Cat scribbled furious capital letters across a sheet of paper and held it up.

I DIDN'T KNOW YOU'D BE SO STUPID
AS TO COPY THE <u>WRONG</u> ANSWERS.

Lyla hissed, 'How was *I* supposed to know they were wrong?'

Cat rolled her eyes, then after a pause smiled broadly and wrote again in more capitals:

I SHOULD HAVE KNOWN YOU DIDN'T!
XXXX

And they both grinned at each other.

33

DON'T RUN, LYLA SPENCE!

'*Clementine Walters . . . Jemima Somerset . . . Lilac Townsend . . .*'

From the stairs Lyla eyed the pile of in-tray letters and narrowed her eyes as the girls whose names were called stepped forward.

'*Faye Peak . . . Imelda Taylor . . .*'

Lyla watched as Faye opened hers. A group gathered around Faye and she began to read her letter aloud. Lyla ached to be in the centre of a cluster of friends with a letter to read. Break-times were the worst parts of the day because everyone had someone to talk to and letters to read, and sometimes Lyla would hang about Miss Trumpet, and sometimes she'd wander off as if she had far more urgent and interesting things to do and had had so many letters that it didn't matter if none came for her that day.

'*Lyla Spence,*' read Miss Trumpet. Lyla, astonished, hurled herself down the stairs.

'Don't run, Lyla Spence!' called Mary Masters.

Lyla wanted to say something clever to show that she could do as she liked in her own Great Aunt's own house, but more than that she wanted the letter.

'Lyla Spence!' called Miss Trumpet again.

Lyla set off a little slower, eyeing the letter Miss Trumpet held. She stretched out her hand, then saw the postmark and froze.

She looked Miss Trumpet in the eye, fighting to keep the tremor from her voice. 'I don't want it,' she said.

'And what am I to do with it this time, Lyla Spence?'

'Oh, anything you like,' answered Lyla in a light and trailing voice.

'I'll take it,' said Cat instantly, stepping forward. 'I know what to do with it.'

Lyla turned away and bowed her head, hands balled into tight fists, eyes brimming. It wasn't Mop who'd written. Lyla hunched her shoulders and headed back up the stairs, feeling hundreds of pairs of eyes burning into her back.

Cat caught up beside her, tugging at her sleeve and saying in an urgent, anguished voice, 'Look, Lyla – it's *from France.*'

Lyla paused, then shook her head and answered, deliberately casual, 'It's only from Father.' She stomped up the first few stairs, a tiny bit pleased that Cat was still behind her and had clearly decided to talk to her again.

'Something might have happened . . . Lyla, you must open it.'

'No, because he doesn't care about me,' snapped Lyla loud enough that all around might hear. 'Give it to Solomon.'

Cat paused. 'Did you know,' she demanded furiously, 'that Solomon says lots of people would like to have fathers who write to them?'

'Well, I don't care what *Solomon* says.'

'All right. I'll make the plane then,' said Cat. She proceeded to open the envelope and to unfold and refold the letter.

'I'm not surprised her mother doesn't bother much with her,' said Faye very loudly.

Lyla was about to retort viciously, when Cat, smoothly, smilingly, interjected.

'Of *course* her mother bothers with her, and *actually* next month it's her birthday and she'll certainly get something from her then.'

Cat took Lyla's arm and they strode together past Faye, but Lyla looked downcast and a little troubled, because Mop might not remember her birthday and Faye might be even more horrid then.

'Look, Lyla,' said Cat smiling and holding something up that was only distantly recognizable as a fighter plane. 'A Hawker Hurricane, most definitely.'

34

A HAWKER HURRICANE IN THE DAMSON

My darling Lyla,

This is a low point for Britain – I hope the very lowest, and that things will take a turn soon for the better. We have only to be thankful that the majority of men came safely home from Dunkirk. For the rest, the Italians have placed their bet with Germany so as to be on what they think will be the winning side. And Germany herself is preparing to invade the tiny island on which I have left my only daughter, while I am under orders to make my way far away from you, to Egypt. We are surrounded there by German-and-Italian-controlled territories, but we must, at all costs, protect Suez.

I hope you are well and happy. It is rather fun, is it not, to have a school arrive at Furlongs? Dear Ada keeps me posted, but I would so dearly love one day to read some words from you.

It is perhaps for the best that your understanding of the things that happened to us is only partial, but one day you will be ready to know the way things really stand. Until that time and whenever I am able, I will write. I will keep on writing and perhaps one day you will read the things I've written.

Yours always,

Father

35

ICE SKATES

'*I'm not surprised her mother doesn't bother much with her.*'
Faye's words revolved in Lyla's head.

She was going to show Faye Peak. It was her birthday soon, and Mop would write, but Lyla would remind Mop just in case because Mop did need to be reminded about things like birthdays.

Furlongs
Ladywood
North Devon

Dearest Mop,

I get everything wrong. I even copy the wrong answers.

But if you were here, I wouldn't get everything wrong.

The reason I had to copy is that Winnie doesn't know about algebra and lots of other things and because I had to do an exam and because I never ever knew I'd have to do one of those. A week is such a long time if you are in Coventry and no one speaks a single word to you. Now no one likes me except Cat, and she is still a bit cross because of me getting her into Coventry, so now it is mostly just me and Bucket again.

G. A. Ada is very cross about Coventry. She says Coventry is cruel and that she might put the teachers in detention because she says they must have forgotten what it is to be a child. She says no one should ever be a teacher unless they can remember what it is like to be young.

Please don't forget my birthday – it is two weeks away now. It is so lonely if you don't get any letters, and because I don't get letters, people think you don't care about me. Also, if my hair was sort of wavier and blonder it would look like Faye Peak's and then people would like me because everyone likes her. I don't know how you do that though and I don't know how to grow up quicker and there are so many things I need you to tell me.

It is really, really cold now. All the ink in the ink pots freezes, and the water in the jugs, and we are allowed to wear hats as well as mittens in classes and even

*in the dining room. One good thing about the cold is
that I have heard that sometimes in winter the lake
freezes, and we might be allowed to skate.*

*Everyone has written home for their skates, so please,
please will you send mine. I'm all right at ice-skating
and it's easier to make friends if you can be good
at something. You could send them for my birthday
because everyone else gets presents on their birthday.*

I do miss you . . .

The bell sounded. School was all bells and gongs and
having to be in certain places at certain times, and
since Lyla had more tardies than anyone else in her
class, she put down her pen and ran downstairs.

36

SAD AND LONELY AND STRANGE

Lyla meandered along the corridor.

French had not been very successful. Bucket had escaped from Lyla's lap, and Mlle Fremont, known to all as Frou-Frou, had grown hysterical and scandalized and had hopped about and then made Lyla leave the class, and it had taken most of the morning to locate Bucket. On finding him, Lyla had tapped Bucket on the nose and told him he'd been wicked to hide in the housemaid's cupboard because finding a small ferret in a house as large as Furlongs could take a very long time indeed.

Lyla passed Faye – who was, of course, loitering around Mary Masters and the clique of prefects that sat huddled in blankets and scarves in the corridor – and she heard her giggle and whisper.

'See, Mary . . . Lyla's just weird, talking to that *thing* . . . That's another reason she doesn't have any friends . . .'

Lyla didn't hear the rest because she was marching

on. She *wouldn't* mind what Faye said, because there was no point in minding about people you didn't like.

She reached the Yellow Silk Room and hesitated. The door was a fraction open, which was odd because she always left it shut. Warily she eyed the room, saw her latest, unfinished letter on the desk and walked very slowly towards it, her heart thumping. Across the bottom of the letter in someone else's handwriting were scrawled the words:

SAD AND LONELY AND STRANGE

Lyla's throat constricted. Her hot, trembling fingers clutched at the paper – what had they read? She imagined them right now whispering and nudging one another, the painful things she'd written passing from ear to ear.

> *Please don't forget my birthday – it is two weeks away now. It is so lonely if you don't get any letters, and because I don't get letters, people think you don't care about me. Also, if my hair was sort of wavier and blonder it would look like Faye Peak's and then people would like me because everyone likes her.*

Lyla writhed with a shame so intense, so physical, that it compelled her to hurl herself on to the bed and kick out and kick out again. She snatched the covers over her head, hugging herself in a welter of rage, then flung them off, rolled over and flung out her arms and legs and beat them on the cover, then writhed and kicked again, the words she'd written reverberating in her head and mingling inside her with some deeper thing that she couldn't bring into the light.

37

ROBIN

'Lyla . . . Lyla . . .'

Lyla was still in bed, her back firmly to the door. 'Go away!'

'It's me – Cat!'

Lyla didn't care who it was. 'Go away!'

There was no sound of footsteps retreating, so Lyla grew suspicious and twisted her head a little and saw that Cat stood in the doorway.

'Go away, Cat.'

'Actually, I won't,' Cat answered in an even, smiling way. 'I just want to say I know what they did, and it isn't right.'

'Who was it?' spat Lyla, sitting up. She flung off the bed cover and glared at Cat. Then she slumped, shaking and sobbing in a broken heap. 'They know everything – *everything* . . . and how would *they* feel if *I* knew everything about *them* – I don't go into *their* rooms and read *their* letters . . .'

'No –' Cat's voice was amused again – 'but

you *do* try on their clothes.'

That made Lyla feel guilty on top of everything else, so she said nothing.

Cat came to the bed and sat by Lyla. 'My mother says she might come down one day, you know, to visit.'

Lyla tensed. She tried to imagine Mop coming and standing at the gate of Furlongs and was suddenly not at all certain that she'd want her to. After a while she asked, 'What sort of shoes does your mother wear?'

'That's a funny sort of question,' said Cat, startled.

'I mean – are they brown and sort of –' Lyla made a shape with her hands – 'sort of clumpy?'

Cat giggled. 'Well, actually, yes – they're very sensible sorts of shoes. Shoes for *doing things* in. She says you have to be able to *do things* in shoes – that that's the whole point of them.'

'What does she *do* in her shoes?' asked Lyla, giggling too, because even she knew this was an odd question.

'You're really very funny. No else asks what shoes Mother wears.'

'Does she do lots of knitting?' asked Lyla.

Cat laughed again. 'Well, yes, but it doesn't matter what shoes she does her knitting in. She sends the knitting to the Red Cross – jerseys and socks and things.'

'So does mine,' said Lyla a little too loud and a little too fast. 'She knits all those things too and she sends them to the Red Cross.'

Cat watched Lyla thoughtfully but said nothing, so after a while Lyla asked, 'Anyway, why do you want to be my friend when no one else does?'

'Oh, well, I don't particularly,' Cat teased, but she stopped smiling when she saw the hurt and shock on Lyla's face. She took Lyla's hands. 'People do think you're a bit odd, you know, but I don't think you're odd. I think you're funny and sweet and brave and unusual.'

Lyla beamed. She liked all of those words. Three out of four of them, anyway. It was only *unusual* that she wasn't so sure about.

Cat paused, then sighed, took a paper from her pocket and said, 'Anyway, I don't like people being mean.' She unfolded the paper. 'Listen to this,' she said, and began to read.

'*Dear Cat,*

The boys here are horrid and won't talk to me. It's becos I read books. They just play silly games like football but I am no good at that becos my glasses go foggy so no one ever wants me on their team. They stole my pockit money and tore the pages of my book. It was Treasure Island *that you gave me. Everyone else knows how to*

make friends even if they haven't been at a bording
school before but I don't.

Love,
Robin'

Cat lowered the letter and sighed. 'Robin's only eight. So that's why I'm here – because I don't like everyone being horrid to one person.'

'Then you don't *actually* like me at all?'

'Well, you're not very easy to like,' said Cat, gentle and teasing.

'Is it because I'm different?'

Cat laughed. 'You're not really different, silly. Everyone's different to everyone else. Don't you see, that's the joy of the whole thing.' Cat leaned a little closer to Lyla. 'Maybe you should just worry less and think less about yourself.'

'I don't think about myself,' said Lyla abruptly. She paused before adding, 'Anyway, certain things about me ARE different.'

'Which things?' asked Cat, still gentle and teasing.

Just how she was different was too painful to force into words, so Lyla remained silent and watched Cat fold the letter and shove it back into her pocket, thinking it would be nice to have a brother send you letters.

'Sometimes . . .' Lyla began, struggling to voice

what she felt. 'Sometimes I feel like I am young on the outside, but all grown up and old on the inside.'

Cat, about to snort with laughter, saw the scowling, tear-stained face beside her, and searched about instead for something helpful to say. 'Well, you may be grown up in some sorts of ways, but not in most ways.'

'Did *you* read the letter?' demanded Lyla.

'No, of course I didn't. I never would.'

And Lyla knew that it was true, that Cat was true to her core and would never read a letter that wasn't meant for her.

38

LYLA'S BIRTHDAY

At the top of the stairs, Lyla hesitated. It was Saturday, her birthday, and she was sure there'd be something from Mop. Eyeing the box, she clopped down in Wicker's too-big shoes. An excited crowd was gathered around Trumpet because of one large, dark green parcel that was too big for the in tray. Lyla gasped. *Harrods.* That could be from Mop, even though Mop didn't generally shop at Harrods.

How nice it would be when her name was read out, and how surprised Faye would be. So, trying to look as though she had many other absorbing things to do, Lyla sauntered down the stairs, plumped herself into a nearby chair, and waited.

'*Jennifer Fraser . . . Daisy Saunders . . . Jane Higgins . . .*'

Lyla could see the in tray dwindling, and still her own name had not come. Too agitated now to pretend otherwise, she rose. She would go and wait beside Miss Trumpet for Mop's parcel.

'It's my birthday,' she told Trumpet.

'Yes, dear. Happy birthday . . .' Trumpet turned at last to the green box. 'Faye Peak, one for you again.'

That box was for Faye.

The crowd of girls around Trumpet swirled and re-formed like a new constellation around Faye – and Lyla, alone, outside the circle, trembled with shock. Transfixed by the sight of Faye Peak with the parcel, she stared as Faye opened it, slowly and pausing at each layer of crisp, rustling tissue to enjoy the attention she was commanding, and then, finally, quite certain of the gasps of envy that would surely come, she lifted the final layer of tissue to reveal a deep-purple satin dress.

Still shaking, Lyla turned back to Miss Trumpet. She saw there were still three letters in Trumpet's hand, so she edged towards her. 'It's my birthday,' she whispered. 'I'm sure Mother's written . . .' Lyla's voice grew uncertain and trailed away because Faye, who was holding up her beautiful dress for all to see, and still had her circle close around her, was listening to Lyla and watching.

Lyla looked at Trumpet, almost pleading with her silently to give her a letter, any letter, to show that someone had remembered her. Trumpet saw Lyla's eyes and she hesitated, then sighed and quickly flicked through the three remaining envelopes.

'No, I'm sorry – they're all for Accounts.'

Lyla blinked furiously, valiantly fighting back her tears, then said in a voice that was loud and bright and brittle, 'Probably it'll come tomorrow then.'

She heard Faye say, 'See, no one ever writes – not even on her birthday. I was told they just dumped her here, you know. I mean, even her mother doesn't want her.'

Lyla fled, stumbling towards the stairs. Cat grabbed at her hand but Lyla pulled herself free, ran blindly on and found herself colliding, at the foot of the stairs, with her great aunt. 'Lyla –' murmured Ada, trying to take Lyla's hands.

But Lyla again pulled herself away and staggered up the stairs.

'Miss Trumpet, what is happening?' demanded Ada. 'This won't do at all, not at all. Explain what is going on.'

Lyla, now at the top of the stairs, didn't care what anyone said to anyone any more.

Alone in her room, she rushed to the desk and flung herself into the chair and picked up a pen to write to Mop, but as she stared at the blank sheet of paper in front of her Faye's voice rang in her ears. *I was told they just dumped her here, you know. I mean, even her mother doesn't want her.*

Lyla paused then bent her head over the paper and began to write, knowing as she did so that a part of herself had changed, that the very deepest part of her had crystallized, had become icy and sharp, and wanted to hurt the person she most loved.

To Mother,

You never write to me and that makes me think you do not love me and that no one ever will. I don't know if you know how hard it is to be always alone and have no one that loves you. I so want to be loved and I don't know if that feeling will ever go away because I think all children need to be loved by their parents.

I will never write to you again.

Your daughter,

Lyla

She sealed the envelope, lifted her head, rose from her desk and walked steadily down to the Hall, where she placed the letter in the out tray beside Old Alfred.

39

SUNDAY

After chapel every Sunday, once they'd hung their long Sunday cloaks in their wardrobes and returned to the Painted Hall, came letter writing, when for an hour the girls were expected to write, as best they could sat cross-legged on the floor, the mandatory weekly letter home.

As so often, that Sunday Lyla sat apart from the rest of her year group, her back turned to the room. When Trumpet handed her a sheet of writing paper, she picked up her pen and, frowning and biting her lips in concentration and trying to recollect the sort of normal things one might say in a letter, she began to write.

She folded and sealed the letter, went to the out tray and carefully slipped her envelope in amidst the pile. Then she turned and walked slowly upstairs, dreading the rest of the day, for Sunday afternoons were long and lonely, and that afternoon Lyla was – as always – alone.

Cat was Lyla's friend, but Cat had other friends too, and they had all made other plans that didn't include Lyla. Everyone always seemed to be doing things without her. Sometimes she would take Violet for a walk along the corridors and to the ballroom to exercise her, and sometimes she would just wander the corridors alone and make herself available in case anyone should see her and ask her to join them. There was, of course, always Brenda. Brenda was always on her own, but Brenda never went to Ladywood and never talked to anyone unless she had to.

The corridors were very long, and sometimes Lyla counted her steps, and sometimes she got bored of counting because it took so many footsteps to get anywhere and you could forget even a very important thing from one end of a corridor to the other.

That afternoon Lyla first went to exercise Violet in the ballroom, and Violet was company of a sort, and then she went to see Sir Galahad. He was the first in the line of suits of armour in the corridor. He and his men were rather companionable really. You grew fond of people you walked past every day, and if you were bored you even gave them names. Lyla placed her palm on Galahad's forearm and paused in a queenly sort of way, then nodded briefly to each as she passed . . . Lancelot, Percival, Tristan, Boris, Garth . . . and as she went, she was thinking of Tuesday.

40

TUESDAY

At break-time on Tuesday, Lyla decided that Trumpet's heart must be bigger than she'd thought, for as Lyla was queuing for milk and biscuits, Trumpet sought her out and said clearly so that lots of people would hear, 'It's come for you – the letter you wanted has come. Isn't that nice?'

Lyla smiled gratefully and reached for the envelope.

'Oh, Lyla, that's wonderful.' Cat had come and was standing by her.

Lyla turned and smiled and reached for her milk and biscuit.

'Well, hurry, open it . . .' said Cat.

'Oh, yes. Shall I read it to you?'

Cat looked a little surprised, but Lyla was determined. She finally had a letter to read, and since everyone read their letters out loud, she would do the same. And so, clutching her glass of powdered milk and her Fox's ginger biscuit, Lyla led Cat to a corner, sat down and unfolded her letter and, glancing up to make sure Faye had seen that she had both a friend and a letter, began to read, loudly enough for Faye to hear.

> 'My darling Lyla,
>
> I haven't sent you any lovely parcels because London is very dangerous just now and I've had to spend so much time in the Anderson shelter. I never go to the Ritz or to the Café de Paris or any of those places where the wrong sorts of people go.'

Cat, who had been half listening, half trying to finish some French Prep, raised her head and began to listen intently. Lyla was pleased and read on:

> 'I do hope that you have a friend who will help you carry Violet's buckets up and down – things are so much more fun in pairs.'

Lyla glanced at Cat. It would be nice if Cat did keep her company with that sometimes.

> 'I do lots of ambulance driving and nursing, but I do so, so long to see you and to hear how everything is going at school. I am already so busy looking for your Christmas present. It probably wouldn't be a purple dress because that is a vulgar colour for a young girl,

but I hope it will arrive safely because so many things get lost in the post in wartime.

All my love,

Mother'

41

GARDEN HILL SCHOOL FOR GIRLS

The term wore on, the staff growing increasingly tense and drawn, murmuring to one another in hushed voices the things they'd heard on the wireless. The prime minister was a worried man. As a nation, we would fight to the last man and the last woman. Britain was fighting on all fronts. Germany wanted to conquer the whole of continental Europe from the Atlantic to Moscow; but Britain had the largest navy; she would be all right.

There was no longer any talk of any girl returning to London. The city was burning. Fires were raging over the East End chemical factories, the skies lit up night after night by the flames. Parents wrote that they were sleeping under their stairs or on the platforms of the London Underground, that the sky went black at times with the number of German planes overhead.

A new duty called 'roof-spotting' was suddenly introduced to the timetable, and a new duty roster pinned to the noticeboard in the hall. Roof-spotting meant long hours on the roof, two girls at a time, watching the skies for German planes.

The summer wore on – the girls were kept busy with lessons as though there was no summer break at all.

Then one morning in October, Pinnacle told the girls that she had to be away for a short while in London, and that Miss Threadgold would step in. The girls sighed and rolled their eyes at one another. *Threadgold.*

Pinnacle returned two days later, subdued and saddened. She was reported by Imelda, who made it her business to know such things, to have entered the Billiard Room and been closeted there a long while with Lyla's Great Aunt Ada.

The following morning at assembly, the Pinnacle made an announcement.

'It is with deep regret that I have to inform you that the beautiful old buildings of our school, the buildings for which I fought with my every atom, were bombed by the Luftwaffe. Almost nothing remains.'

There was a collective intake of breath, then silence. After a while, someone began to sob, louder perhaps than was strictly necessary, and it was of course Faye Peak, who was always conscious that tears could make you the centre of attention.

'I am only glad that none of you were in those buildings; that we have the good fortune to be here.'

Pinnacle lifted her head. 'But remain assured, we will go on. This school has been my life's work. I will fight for it and for you all, for the spirit of a school does not lie in its buildings. Be in no doubt, Hitler will soon find that the British are not like other nations – the British cannot easily be beaten.' She paused. 'And Garden Hill School for Girls is, of course, fortunate to be here at Furlongs, fortunate that our hostess is allowing us to remain here for the duration of the war, and until such a moment as I am in a position to rebuild the school.'

A ruckus erupted in the Painted Hall, girls hugging and kissing one another, and Lyla looked about, astonished that everyone should be so pleased. Pinnacle cast her eyes about the hall and smiled a grim, quiet smile.

42

A HAWKER TYPHOON
IN THE DAMSON

My dear Lyla,

*Are there still blackberries at Furlongs? Does the gorse
still roll and swell and blaze like a yellow sea? Those
were golden years for me, Lyla, and I long to hear
you're happy there, that you swim at Shearwater,
that you skate on the lake in winter and picnic in the
bracken in summer.*

*Did I tell you Solomon was my servant – batman,
they call them in the army – in the last war? I think
not – you weren't in a talking frame of mind when I
drove you down to Furlongs. Solomon's a gentleman
to the core. There was no pension for the wounded
after the last war, no work for a man with a wooden
leg, so it was Ada, of course, who took him in. He
would lay down his life, I think, for your Great
Aunt Ada.*

Do watch out for her inventions – they're not entirely safe. When I was a boy, she blew up her own glasshouses with a remarkable long-range projectile that she lobbed rather casually out of the window of the Billiard Room as she sipped her whiskey and read The Times.

I think of you so often. And of Ada, dear Ada. Have you grown fond of her? She has the heart of a Crusader, the will of a tornado, the vigour of a Viking . . . but she'd never remember to eat or do any of the small, ordinary things in life were it not for Solomon being there to remind her.

Let's hope America will join the war. At least all the contestants would then be in the ring, the gloves off, and we would stand an even chance.

Lyla, do – sometimes – think of me, for if I fight, I fight for you.

Yours always,

Father

43

ROSE AND SILVER

That Friday morning, a most strange apparition was observed on the drive, for a very large, dark green box appeared to be making its way up it almost entirely of its own accord; appeared, that is, until one spotted the intrepid lace-up boots of Mabel Rawle, the postmistress, poking out beneath it.

At break-time, an excited crowd gathered about the mail table, but Lyla sat alone once more, determined to be not at all interested in the largest box that had ever arrived for a Garden Hill girl. She opened a notepad and took out a pen to busy herself so she could block out the names of all the girls getting letters from their mothers, and to show that she didn't need packages from the people that loved her.

Miss Trumpet, relishing the attention and suspense of the girls, left the green box till last before finally looking up and reading aloud, her eyebrows arched in pleasure and surprise, 'Miss Lyla Spence.'

Notepad and pencil spilling from her lap, Lyla

leaped up and pushed her way through to Miss Trumpet. The girls withdrew into a cautious, distant circle, nudging one another and raising eyebrows.

'Lyla Spence, is this a thing you'll actually be wanting?'

'Of course I want it. It's from Mother,' said Lyla as if Miss Trumpet were half-witted.

It was postmarked 'Knightsbridge' and Lyla wondered that Mop had gone to Harrods, for she generally shopped in Selfridges. She took the parcel and walked slowly back across the hall so everyone could see just how big it was, how she had a mother that loved her, just like everyone else did, and who sent her lovely things and thought of her every day.

She positioned herself on the edge of her chair, remembering how Faye had unwrapped her dress and thinking, *Very slowly, so everyone can see.*

Under the last layer of white tissue was the softest and silkiest of dresses, rose-coloured, embroidered with trailing silver honeysuckle and white butterflies, with a silver sash to tie at the back of the waist. Tears came to her eyes for she'd never seen a thing of such sweetness in a dress before, and an unlikely picture came to her mind of Mop clambering over all the rubble in all the streets of London to trawl all the shops for the prettiest dress. She looked up at the circle that surrounded her and held it out so they could feel the silky weightlessness of it, and she saw

Great Aunt Ada beside Solomon at the foot of the stairs, both of them watching.

Since Lyla had a circle around her, she picked out the card from the box and read aloud: '*Dear Lyla, I decided on rose and silver for you, as those colours are so fresh and delicate. Purple –*' Lyla hesitated, and read on a little quieter – '*Purple is, of course, quite wrong. Love, Mother.*'

When Lyla looked up, Cat was frowning slightly and staring at the dress, and Faye Peak and Mary were whispering together. Cat stretched out a hand to touch the dress and said quietly, 'Lucky you, Lyla.'

Mary said loudly to Faye, 'It's not as if anyone would ever ask her to a party anyway, she doesn't really have any friends. When would she even wear it?'

But Lyla didn't care because Mop had finally sent her something and it wasn't just a letter. Clutching the dress, she rose and ran over to her great aunt and held it out. 'Look – isn't it the prettiest thing you ever saw?' In a tumble, she burbled on, 'I knew Mop would send something wonderful. And she always has the best taste and chooses the prettiest things and knows all the cleverest places.'

'Of course, dear,' murmured Ada, before turning away.

Solomon, however, stuck his chest out and beamed and said how Harrods was a marvellous store with very helpful staff. Lyla was touched that he should be so pleased for her and never wondered at all how Solomon might know about the staff in Harrods.

Lyla hung that dress from the end of her bed so she'd see it last thing at night and first thing in the morning, and even if she never got another parcel or letter ever, she'd have that dress, which Mop had chosen for her, and which must surely be the prettiest in all of England.

44

THE TRUCE

Once again it was Imelda who knew what was going on. She had a weaselly way of watching and digging things up, titbits of scandal or gossip that she used as currency among her peers. *If you are my friend, I will tell you things that other people don't know.*

'The Pinnacle isn't coming back! I heard Threadgold saying so,' she whispered.

The girls sat on the floor of the Painted Hall waiting for assembly. They'd been kept there a while and had grown restive, feverish speculations running from ear to ear.

After what seemed a very long while, when the girls had become more restless and the speculations even wilder, Great Aunt Ada appeared on the landing, her face grave and drawn.

'The night before last, London suffered what might prove to be one of the worst nights of the Blitz.' She raised a hand to quieten the ensuing murmurs. 'There's no cause for concern. We have made great efforts to contact your families and to ascertain that they are all safe.' With a visible effort she raised her head higher and said, 'Miss Pinnacle, however, shall, for a short while, be standing aside as headmistress, for her son, Richard, was among those who lost his life that night.'

Absolute silence descended upon the hall.

Richard. Pinnacle had a son. Lyla's Great Aunt had been right. There was a mystery to Pinnacle after all. An unmarried woman with a son. Lyla glanced at her great aunt, but Ada's head was deeply bowed.

'I have decided that I will step in to fill the gap.'

The senior staff shuffled and coughed and the girls raised their heads and gawped, but Lyla's great aunt drew herself up to her full height as if to dismiss all doubts.

'Night after night, the Luftwaffe have attacked our cities, our ports and our industries. Every day and night for eleven weeks. One third of London has been destroyed, twenty-nine thousand killed, a further twenty-six thousand wounded. But today, all our thoughts are with dear Pinnacle, who has lost her only son.'

Dear Pinnacle? wondered Lyla. Has there been a sea change in their dealings with one another?

'Poor old Pinnacle. It's going to be fun, though, with your aunt in charge,' Cat whispered as they rose. But Lyla pursed her lips in apprehension at what her aunt might have in store.

45

AVERAGES AND PERCENTAGES

Great Aunt Ada stood at Threadgold's desk and surveyed the class.

'Threadgold's teeth are decidedly *rickety* – yes, rickety – so I have arranged for her to visit the dentist in Ladywood each Monday at this hour, as a matter of *urgency*. So you see, as Threadgold will be in Ladywood every Monday, I shall be taking this class. Moreover, Pinfold is in London, and in her absence I have decided that changes must be made. Yes. Changes. Things must be fair. Reports, results, prizes and so forth – they must go both ways, must they not?'

Warily, Lyla flipped her pencil between her forefingers, for, judging by the twinkling in her aunt's eyes, some mischief was afoot.

'Now, averages will be the subject for today. We'll give them a *practical* application to demonstrate their usefulness, because that's only fair. You see, I shall never encumber you with knowledge you shan't need.' Ada went about placing a piece of paper on each desk. 'Down the left-hand side you'll see the names of your teachers, and across the top a list of indispensable skills. Now, you will each place a mark out of twenty in each of those five boxes and then you'll add them to produce a total score out of one hundred, a percentage for that particular teacher.'

The girls raised their heads and caught each other's eyes, some horrified, some delighted. Lyla read the headings along the top:

Enthusiasm
Effort
Encouragement
Subject Knowledge
Ability to Inspire

'You may, of course, decline to participate in the exercise,' continued Aunt Ada, 'but that's not at all in your best interests. This exercise is confidential. Then – and this is the fun part – we will add up all the scores you fifteen girls have given Nodding, for example, and then divide that total by fifteen, and there you have it – the average percentage she has been awarded by her pupils.'

One or two brave girls took up their pencils.

Ada grew very fierce. 'They must be judged too, must they not? They are on trial as much as you are, and who better to assess the quality of their teaching than their pupils, hmm?'

Cat grinned at Lyla and took up her pencil. Lyla took hers too, and began by giving Nodding a score of five out of twenty for *Ability to Inspire* because she never said what the point of geography was, nor how estuaries and and deltas and oil wells actually affected the people who lived on them, and that was surely the point of the subject. Lyla glanced around and saw that everyone was grinning and rushing to write numbers in all the boxes.

'Quick, quick, marvellous – now fold them up like ballot papers and pop them into my pockets.' Aunt Ada went about the room, and the girls tucked their papers into the various pockets that ran up and down her person.

'Let's start with geography and Miss Nodding: oh dear. Miss Nodding seems not to be doing as well as she might. Let's see, now write this down: thirty per cent, plus forty-one per cent, dear dear, plus fifteen per cent . . . I see her grades are consistently poor – you are all broadly in agreement. Yes, yes, what fun. Add up all the percentages you have individually awarded Nodding and then divide that by the number of girls in the class, fifteen. Yes, so divided by fifteen, what do we have? Who has the answer?'

Lyla's hand shot up and she answered gleefully (on account of Noddy not knowing the whole point of geography and always sounding as though she were

): 'Thirty-three per cent.'

right. Oh dear, yes, *Could try harder, more enthusiasm required*, do we think? Only thirty-three per cent overall for poor Miss Nodding.'

As Great Aunt Ada proceeded through her table of results, Lyla looked around the class, thinking that it was a pity that all lessons didn't speed by quite so amusingly as this one and how engaged everyone was by averages and percentages.

As they rose to leave, all whispering and nudging one another, Great Aunt Ada's eyes were twinkling as she said, 'I understand marks are exhibited publicly, are they not, at Garden Hill School for Girls? What fun.'

46

RELLIES

There was a most unusual aspect to assembly the following morning, for not a single member of staff was present. The prefects looked around, bewildered and unnerved.

Great Aunt Ada breezed past Lyla at the top of the stairs and murmured, 'It all makes for most interesting reading. Most interesting.' She smiled, delighted at her wickedness and at the excited nodding and pointing and whispering that was going on below. 'D'you see, it is most important that the staff are reminded what it is to be a child.'

Lyla then saw the dreaded School Examination Board results had been replaced with Great Aunt Ada's averages and percentages results from yesterday's class. She turned to her and whispered, deeply shocked, 'Where're the staff? Have they seen it?'

'Oh, dear me – I nearly forgot. Solomon! Solomon! Ah, good, Solomon, you may release them now. You see –' she turned to Lyla – 'they're in the Undercroft,

appens – in detention, as it were. Yes,
air-raid siren was sounded early this
ugh, somewhat mysteriously, it was
the Staffroom, and Solomon had
temporarily mislaid the key.' She dug about in her
shin pocket and eventually unearthed a large iron key.

'She's rather marvellous, your aunt,' Cat said to Lyla
as they peered at the staff marks on the noticeboard.

'No, she's not; she's just embarrassing,' hissed Lyla.
She looked down at the ground, immediately aware of
her disloyalty.

'Oh, *all rellies* are embarrassing. Mummy does
mortifying things like talking to bus drivers. She'll just
stop her motor simply anywhere – say, the middle
of Knightsbridge – just because she likes the look
of someone.' Cat mimicked her mother. *"Oh – do
look at that nice man, such a kind sort of face, do look,
darling, shall we ask him what he's doing for Christmas? He
probably doesn't have anyone at all, you know."* But then
of course it turns out the bus driver does in fact have
a family, and a Christmas pudding, and doesn't want
Mummy's ones at all.'

'That's not embarrassing,' said Lyla.

'Only because she's not *your* mother, but if you were
queuing at the post-office counter and she suddenly
began to sing the descant part of something – you
know, a hymn or something – but with all the words
in a muddle–'

'Does she *really* sing descants in post offices?'

'Oh yes, and if we're on a beach, she'll look about and just choose some people she likes the look of: "*Do look, darling, the ones with the red sunshade – we'll just go and join them, shall we?*" So off we go to join some perfectly bewildered strangers who don't want us there at all, while Mother says, "*Do – oh, do, just help me rig up this umbrella, and this here's young Catharine – she's just the same age as your little person there . . .*"'

Lyla was thinking how sad it was never to have been taken to beaches by her own mother because of the coarsening effect of salt water on the complexion until she remembered they had been been talking first of all about how embarrassing Great Aunt Ada was, so she said, 'Well, at least your mother doesn't put the staff in detention and lock them in the Undercroft.'

47

ROOF-SPOTTING

Lyla and Cat sat together on the roof one cold Sunday afternoon, wrapped and muffled in scarves and blankets, glancing very occasionally up to an empty sky. Lyla toyed with the handle of the red air-raid siren that must be sounded should they spot a German aeroplane as she contemplated the scene.

'It's not as if the Germans would even bother to come here,' she muttered.

Cat looked at Lyla for a long while before saying, 'You're always so cross. Why?'

'You would be too if the things that happen to me happened to you.'

'What has actually happened to you, Lyla?'

Lyla turned away and thought back and knew she couldn't remember everything, only fragments.

Alone in the drawing room on the night that had turned out to be her last at Lisson Square, Lyla had fingered the scarf Mop had let drop on the centre table. Shocked by the slithery chill of it, she'd replaced it, carefully, trying to achieve Mop's artful alchemy, the touch she had that could turn tin to silver. As the gramophone had turned to a slow dance and the gloss had slid away into the dusk, Lyla had wandered about Mop's drawing room, alone, amidst the empty glasses.

Even now, although it had been so long since she'd last seen or spoken to her mother, the voice that was always clearest in her head, the voice that accompanied her everywhere and shaped her entire world, was always Mop's.

Sitting on the rooftop with Cat, Lyla tightened the blanket around her shoulders and glanced up at the sky as she struggled to put what she remembered into words. 'Father was always unkind. He was cold. Mop says he'd've killed her with his coldness,' she said eventually.

Lyla remembered how Mop, as she'd absently rearranged the tulips on the centre table, had said to one of her guests, 'Do you know Lovell's found some sad little place to live in – grim and sunless and grey as Welsh shingle.' Mop had giggled and said how there were only books in it – books and upright wooden chairs made specially to be uncomfortable, by Methodists, because they were the chairs you liked if you happened to have Welsh blood.

Lyla glanced at Cat and said, 'He made her very unhappy because he thinks with his head not with his heart.'

'Did he leave her?'

'Yes,' snapped Lyla, somewhat aggressively, because she had discovered it was easier to admit some things (both to herself and to Cat) than it was to admit others. So she answered as best she could. 'He left her and he left me. He made her unhappy and then he left us.'

'How old were you?'

'I don't know . . . three maybe, or four—'

'If you were only four, then you can't remember anything . . . How do you know he made her unhappy?'

'Because that's what Mop told me. She said Father ran off with a horrid woman from Brighton called Ethel because he didn't love us any more.'

Cat, watching Lyla carefully, hesitated before she asked, 'But you don't know for sure, do you, that he doesn't love you? Nor about Ethel?'

Lyla frowned. *No one understood anything at all. No one understood the things that had happened to Lyla Spence.*

Cat was steady and gentle and persistent. 'When you were kidnapped, how did he actually steal you without your mother noticing? Wasn't she in the house?'

Lyla turned her back on Cat, rounded her shoulders and hissed, 'Of course she was there . . .' She broke off, and a frown formed on her brow and eventually she said. '. . . It hurts when I remember, it hurts and it aches and I get confused about everything and, anyway, I'm not going to talk about it any more.'

48

THE GERMAN SHIPPING

The following week, Great Aunt Ada embarked with gusto and enthusiasm on some rather eccentric adjustments to the curriculum.

'These are terrible times. You must be on guard. You must not be encumbered by knowledge you don't need – French, and so on. No, no, you must be prepared for the worst; you must be practical and prepared. When the German shipping comes up the Bristol Channel, we shall be ready for it, shall we not?' She looked dolefully at the baffled faces of girls who thought they'd been evacuated so as to be out of harm's way. 'We shall learn how to use air-raid sirens. We shall continue to patrol the skies for German aircraft. We shall be prepared. Above all, we shall be prepared.

'What's more, we will think about *human rights, Currants, votes for women, history backwards,* and *first aid.* Yes, yes, and *argument,* that's the thing, *alliteration,* and so forth, *mayhem, mavericks, mischief* – yes. I shall explain it all in due course. We will develop your dreams, increase your curiosity, grow your imagination, and we will do no French, no French at all, for no one of consequence speaks it any longer.' Great Aunt Ada's eyes rested on Frou-Frou, against whose entire nation she now nursed an implacable scorn.

Great Aunt Ada never did explain what 'Currants' or 'history backwards' were, for her eyes alighted then on the basket of hockey sticks in the lobby, and she continued brightly, 'We must be cheerful, we must be prepared and we must be ready for the worst, for we shall do whatever is demanded of us, hmmm? Stand, girls, stand, fall into line – form a column of twos, smallest on the right and tallest on the left.' Great Aunt Ada swept across the hall, gesturing vaguely about. 'Yes, yes, now follow me. Quick, march!'

The girls straggled to their feet and the staff shuffled uncomfortably and glanced at one another, but Ada waved an arm briskly in their direction. 'Yes, yes, you too – we must all be ready, and if the time comes, each and every one of us will do our duty. Hands at your sides. Smartly, right leg – one two, one two, forward march.' In the lobby she snatched up a hockey stick and steamed out, brandishing it with gusto, on to the forecourt. The girls, each now bearing a hockey stick, followed her outside in a wayward crocodile, the staff trailing hesitantly at the far end of the line.

Ada marched her troops round and round the fountain till they were coiled about it like a Catherine wheel.

Keeping the hockey stick smartly under her left arm, she sang a rowdy song, breaking from time to time to bark at those who fell out of step. Then, because she seemed only to know the first verse, she sang that several times over.

Lyla saw that the Garden Hill girls were smiling and enjoying themselves, and as they fell into a new and tidy formation, she scowled and told herself, *They just do what anyone tells them to.*

'Halt. About-turn. Salute. Yes, yes, very good.'

Ada, standing at the centre in front of the girls, fell back two paces and clicked her heels, and everyone copied her, just like a game of Simon Says.

'Take aim.'

She raised her hockey stick and levelled it the unseen enemy.

'Fire!'

After a while Ada decided that the enemy had fled and that it was all very satisfactory and she began to declaim some rousing Shakespeare that belonged to another war entirely.

Then she herded the regiment of rosy-cheeked, chattering girls and hobbling staff back into the Painted Hall, plumped herself down on to her chair and firmly shook open *The Times.*

49

ISLANDS

The following Monday, Lyla's class once again enjoyed the dubious benefits of Threadgold's weekly visit to the dentist in Ladywood.

'Dreaming deepens the soul,' Great Aunt Ada began fiercely, her eyes fixing on each girl in turn. 'Dreaming is how you discover what sort of person you want to be. If you don't dream, hmmm, you'll end up being quite the wrong sort of person for *you*, d'you see? Certain grown-ups –' Ada narrowed her eyes – 'are telling you to be a certain sort of person, but you may well want to be an entirely different sort of person. That is why you must allow your dreams to ramble, like –'Aunt Ada cast about for inspiration – 'like climbing roses. Or skylarks. Yes, yes – to soar, like skylarks.'

Lyla glowered at her desk. Why couldn't Great Aunt Ada be more like other people's aunts?

'Outside, girls – chop-chop. No, no scarves, Brenda, for the Greeks have need of them.' Great Aunt Ada steamed down the corridor. 'One two, one two, no Brenda, no hats. They're a great impediment to clear thinking.'

The girls hurried to keep pace with Great Aunt Ada, gathering around her on the lawn, waiting for her next pronouncement.

'Yes, over there.' She gestured vaguely about. 'Empty your heads, fill your minds with dreams, as sponges with water.'

Lyla looked around surreptitiously to discover what Garden Hill girls thought of Great Aunt Ada's approach to education, for this wasn't like the classes other teachers gave. But their heads were tilted up, eyes shut, and only Imelda was looking about, her mouth half open as if dreams might enter her head that way, because there didn't seem to be anything in Imelda's head unless someone put it there for her. Lyla quickly turned her own face upward to show Imelda that Lyla Spence was fit to burst with the dreams that were inside her head.

And soon enough, thoughts of Mop were drifting about in Lyla's head, and she dreamed how one day she'd be just like Mop. Then she thought perhaps she wouldn't wear her hair like a lampshade or such trailing clothes. Perhaps she wouldn't have such a careful, tidy house as Mop's either. No, she would live on an island. Lyla's dream of an island blossomed and spread, and soon she was floating among a sea of islands because a world had come into her head in which every child had their own island, and they lived there with only their parents and the people who loved them, and everyone on every island wore grass skirts.

'To your desks, girls! Don't waste time – take your seats and quickly write down your dreams before they run away. Be brief. Brevity encourages clarity of thought and vision. We don't want to waste anyone's time, do we now?'

Aunt Ada plonked her slippered feet on to Threadgold's desk.

The girls glanced uncertainly at one another. Lyla smiled to herself and began:

Mothers will always be with the children they belong to and never become separated. There will be no wars, and there will be no women called Ethel.

Soon the words were racing across her page.

'Good, good,' said Great Aunt Ada abruptly. 'Your papers, girls. Your papers.' She gestured vaguely about the room.

The girls rose, clutching their papers. Imelda was always first to do anything a teacher asked, so she placed her paper beside Aunt Ada's velvet slippers.

'No, no!' barked Aunt Ada, scandalized.

Imelda started with fear.

'Not for *me*, Imelda – for the *chimney*. Those dreams are an entirely private matter, for yourselves, girls, not for me.' Aunt Ada lifted *The Times* but continued to expound aloud to the baffled class. 'Yes, the chimney. That is a most convenient place for all concerned, is it not?'

Aunt Ada's mind had drifted, for she shook *The Times* in the satisfied kind of way that denoted she felt she had caused enough mischief for the morning.

50

PINK DANDELIONS

'Outside, girls – chop-chop. Coats on, over your bed jackets. It is a high and starry night, just the right kind of night.' Great Aunt Ada was making sweeping movements with her arms across the Painted Hall and all those that were gathered in it for evening prayer, shooing them and the cowed staff outside.

'Tomorrow I will launch my *invention* classes, and by way of preparation I'll show you a small sideline of my own: my Dandelions – my very own fireworks. They're just a minor by-product of my own inventions. They were created, d'you see, to protect us all from the German shipping. Yes, yes, should Hitler dare to send his shipping up the Bristol Channel, he will meet with my Pink Dandelions.' Ada tilted her chin and beamed to indicate that the Pink Dandelions would be – of course, and undoubtedly, and without question – the absolute and irrevocable undoing of the entire German navy.

'Their instruments, don't you see, they won't be

able to use them, won't be able to navigate.' Aunt Ada smiled. 'They'll be befuddled by the lights; they'll run aground on the treacherous rocks of the North Devon coast, oh yes.' Now Great Aunt Ada bellowed towards the currant bushes of the kitchen garden, 'SOLOMON! ON THE COUNT OF THREE, PLEASE. There'll be noise, girls – a lot of noise. Brace yourselves.'

There was an ear-splitting crack, and another, and another – and suddenly rose-coloured fireworks were erupting in the starry sky, bursting into showers that each in turn spawned yet more showers, which burst and spawned, and burst and spawned again – dizzying new constellations spawning new constellations, star after star rising and exploding in luminous showers that cast an other-worldly pink over all the girls, and sheep, and staff.

Ada looked about in satisfaction and, as the last star sank, said, 'Tomorrow, we shall look at *your* inventions. What things can you think of that do not exist today? As we stand here, Great Men in Whitehall are hard at work on all manner of most amusing inventions. Bouncing Bombs. Skipping Bombs. Stink Bombs. Ah yes, the Stink Bomb, a most vicious thing. The men in Whitehall have dreamed up the precise combination of odours that will turn the German forces back to Berlin.'

Great Aunt Ada peered at the girls. 'How wonderful.

A smell that can disperse an army and yet not kill a single man.' Her iridescent eyes twinkled. 'Oh yes, all manner of skulduggery is being dreamed up in the dim caverns of Whitehall.

'But which among you can conceive of things that do not yet exist? Hmm? Motors that propel us to the moon? Telephones that show you the face at the other end? Hmm? Nothing has ever been invented, girls, nothing has ever come into existence that did not first exist in someone's imagination.'

Afterwards Cat asked Lyla, 'How does your aunt know what goes on in Whitehall?'

Lyla answered promptly, 'She doesn't. She's just dotty.'

51

A BETTER WORLD

After the brief Christmas break, classes started once more, and Threadgold's teeth were again required by the dentist in Ladywood.

The girls of Form IV found Great Aunt Ada in a solemn frame of mind. After waiting a good long while, she raised her head, looked about and barked, 'Can you imagine a better world? Hmm? Well, can you? What does it look like?' Another pause. 'Last night Hitler changed the city of Bristol from the City of Churches to the City of Ruins. The Jacobean Hospital destroyed, four ancient churches gone, five thousand incendiary bombs, twelve thousand high explosives, tens of thousands of homes destroyed. Now, you –' Great Aunt Ada peered from girl to girl – 'you are adults-IN-WAITING. There is, in fact, currently *no point* to you at all. For the time being, you have *no purpose*.

'But one day, when we've done away with Hitler, you will rebuild the world. And what kind of world will you build for your children and children's children? Write a CHARTER, girls, for the world you want. Freedom of speech? Women's rights? Votes? Freedom for all from persecution? . . . Equal pay? Equal opportunity? A first-class education for all? Hmm? Chop-chop – pick up your pencils and remember: *brevity*. Brevity encourages clarity of vision. We'll send your charter to the trenches. Yes, yes, our men must be entirely clear what they're fighting for.'

52

GELIGNITE

Cat had told Lyla that she would spend Sunday with her, so Lyla had been looking forward to Sunday all week and was about to suggest going to Ladywood, when Cat said, 'Come on. I want to find out what Aunt Ada is doing.'

'Oh, I already know that – she'll be reading in the Smoking Room. I can tell you what she'll be wearing too, because she wears the same thing every Sunday: tweed plus twos left over, probably, by an ancient retainer.'

'Come on. I think there's a *mystery* about your aunt – and anyway, it's what she's been up to in the Billiard Room that I want to find out.'

So Lyla led Cat down the stone stairs and along the staff passage, rather proud to know her way around all the secret parts of the house. She put a finger to her lips and began to tiptoe. She pushed open the letter box of the Billiard Room door, peeked through it, and saw the bottles of 'Gelignite' and 'Blasting Powder' and wires. Nodding, she gestured to Cat to look in.

Cat peered in for ages, and Lyla began to grow impatient. Finally, Cat crept away from the door a little and whispered with a sense of urgency, 'Do you think it's all quite safe?'

'Oh yes, quite safe,' answered Lyla. 'They're only the Pink Dandelions she showed us that she invented to confuse the German shipping.'

'I see,' said Cat. As they turned and walked away, she added, 'Father realizes he was at Oxford with your Great Aunt Ada. He says it was unusual for a lady to have gone to Oxford to study a science in those days.'

Lyla didn't like people knowing too much about her or her relations. 'I *already* know there's nothing very *usual* about her.'

'You're very *contrary*, Lyla . . .' Cat paused. 'You're the kind of person who goes down the *up* escalators and up the *down* ones. Well . . . you *are*, aren't you?'

'What's wrong with that? Doesn't everyone do that?'

Cat giggled and took her arm and asked if Lyla would come with her to Ladywood that following Sunday, so then Lyla didn't mind about being called contrary.

53

PROBABILITY

Aunt Ada peered dolefully at the formulae on Threadgold's blackboard and murmured, 'Really, it is a miracle that curiosity survives formal education.'

Lyla's classmates watched Ada nervously and braced themselves for another of her unusual stabs in the direction of mathematics.

'Quadratic equations, I see. Did Threadgold explain why she is burdening you with quadratics, hmm? I suppose you've tired of them already, but they weren't entirely invented to deaden the soul. They were invented by the Babylonians, taken up by the Ancient Greeks, and they're used today not only to bore schoolgirls, but by Great Men to calculate World-Changing Things.'

Faye and Imelda exchanged confused glances, as Ada continued.

'Well, girls, Prudence in the kitchen is in need of a clearer understanding of quadratics and of the laws of probability. Pick up the blackboard, girls, take your exercise books, chop-chop, follow me, for we must go to her. Dear Prudence has not removed her tin hat since we declared war on Germany, for she is certain that Hitler is planning to drop a bomb directly on to her pastry table.'

Arriving at the kitchen, Ada flung open the door, and the fourth-formers were presented with the spectacle of the pink-faced Prudence in the aforesaid tin hat, brandishing a rolling pin. Then they saw the cause of Prudence's dismay: handsome Henny trotting about amidst the copper pots and pans and showing no signs of laying an egg.

'Ah, Prudence,' declared Ada.

Prudence's indignation at Henny turned to alarm at the unaccountable appearance of her mistress and so many schoolgirls in her kitchen. 'What's happened? What's going on?' she asked, clamping a hand to her tin in fear at what this sudden invasion by Form IV might portend.

'Now, now, dear Prudence, do sit – nothing untoward is happening. It's only that the girls and I feel you're in need of a clearer understanding of the laws of probability. Yes, yes, the blackboard next to me, please. Now, girls, let's apply the laws of probability to the matter of the bomb and the pastry table.'

Resting their exercise books on said pastry table, the girls made feverish notes, trying to keep pace with Ada's calculations. 'The pastry table is four by four feet, and, yes, girls, that makes sixteen square feet, that goes on the top, draw a line underneath, now convert the United Kingdom into square feet and put that underneath. That's sixty million acres in total. One acre represents forty thousand square feet, so yes, chop-chop, multiply forty thousand by sixty million and what do you have, hmm, what fraction of the overall land mass does Prudence's pastry table represent? . . . Good, now you've done that, take the size of the German bomb, SC 250, the Sprengbombe Cylindrisch, that is, the general-purpose high-explosive carried by German bombers. I am sure you know, do you not, that the Sprengbombe Cylindrisch measures fifteen inches in diameter, so, chop-chop, do the maths, girls, convert fifteen square inches into feet, then put that over the pastry table . . .'

Ada's conversions and fractions and parabolas ran dizzyingly over the edges of the blackboard and up Prudence's walls. Some of the girls, including Faye, were still hastily scribbling down what they could, but Prudence, unimpressed by the procession of numbers across her walls, had nudged off her shoes and set about rubbing her bunions until Ada, with a flourish, concluded her calculations with a number that ran all the way along the top of the primus stove and had so many zeros that you couldn't tell where it started and where it finished.

'Hmm, d'you see, Prudence? So large a number is

meaningless, is it not? We cannot even IMAGINE such a number, cannot envisage even what that number *represents*? No, no, what we need, d'you see, is a *comparison*; only by means of a comparison can we make a thing real to us.'

'So, let us look at the likelihood of, for example, a sheep making her way to the top of the clocktower. For that is as unlikely, is it not, as the matter of a Sprengbombe Cylindrisch landing on Prudence's pastry table?'

With this, Great Aunt Ada launched an entirely new set of calculations relating to the probability of the sheep and the clock tower. A dizzying stream of numbers and letters and brackets made its way across Prudence's walls and finally, mercifully came to a conclusion that happened to be much the same in length as the conclusion of her first calculation, Ada threw down her chalk and said triumphantly, 'D'you see, Prudence? The numbers are roughly the same because, of course, the probability of the sheep and the bomb are roughly *comparable*. So, you see, there's nothing to fear – nothing to fear at all, is there? Oh dear, I see you don't agree . . .'

Prudence, still rubbing her bunions, squinted sceptically at a number that seemed to have neither beginning nor ending.'. . . and of course, in a way, you're quite right,' continued Ada. 'In fact, the problem is that algebra doesn't have *all* the solutions;

it can only take us so far. We must prove the matter of probability *empirically*, yes, yes. Come, dear Prudence – we must go in search of a sheep capable of scaling my clock tower, must we not, in order to be able to imagine just how improbable the matter of the bomb and the sheep actually are.'

At which juncture, Prudence leaped up in delight and waddled over to the copper pans, amidst which, it appeared, Henny had – most improbably – laid an egg.

VESTS AND KNICKERS

When the weather grew warm again, and warmer still, and the summer break finally arrived, Lyla and Cat would often volunteer for roof-spotting.

One afternoon, growing tired of staring into a clear blue sky for German planes, they began to sun themselves and then grew hot, and stripped down to their vests and knickers. They were larking about among the statues of the parapet, striking classical poses and bursting into peals of laughter at each other, when Great Aunt Ada suddenly and most unexpectedly appeared amidst the turrets. Cat and Lyla leaped down and groped about for their clothes as she marched towards them in what appeared to be a state of great agitation.

'Read it,' she announced abruptly, thrusting an envelope into Lyla's hands. 'You cannot continue to ignore your father. I cannot stand by and let this happen – it's too sad. Don't you see? Lovell was like a son to me.' She stalked away, pausing at the little door that led up to the roof, then turned and said with some anger. 'What would you do if his letters stopped coming, Lyla – have you ever thought about that? If one day they just *stopped*?'

Lyla stared at the envelope, then, with determination, thrust it into Cat's hands. 'Give it to Solomon.'

Cat looked stricken and whispered, 'Lyla, Ada knows something, I'm sure she does. That's why she's upset. I think you *need* to read it, otherwise she would just have given it to Trumpet instead of bringing it all the way up here.' She thrust the letter back at Lyla.

Lyla shook her head and turned away.

'Do you even know where he is?' Cat pleaded. 'Do you know what's happening there? He's fighting, Lyla, fighting for England, for *us*.'

'I don't care what happens to him.'

'If my father left me –' Cat spoke carefully – 'I probably wouldn't care what happened to him either. But I don't see that he has *really* left you, since he's always writing.' At the warning look on Lyla's face, Cat placed the envelope deep in the pocket of her skirt but nevertheless she asked, 'Do you look when Solomon throws them out into the tree? Do you even know if they're there next day? Have you ever looked?'

Lyla shook her head.

'They're never there in the morning, Lyla, that's

the thing. They're never there. If you even looked, you'd know.'

'That's just because Tawny doesn't like litter in the park,' said Lyla.

'*I* look for them, you know, because *I* mind. I mind for *you* and I mind for your father and I mind for Solomon, because it makes him so sad – he has tears in his eyes, Lyla, when he folds those letters up.'

'Father *left* *us*!' Lyla suddenly erupted with bitterness. 'He walked out. Left us to go and live in a grey house with hard chairs and a lady from Brighton.'

'Oh, Lyla,' said Cat wearily.

'Shall I read you my letter from Mop?' offered Lyla. She wanted Cat to sit and stay with her and for everything to return to how it was before the letter came.

'No, actually. Not today, thank you,' came Cat's reply.

55

A DE HAVILLAND MOSQUITO
IN THE DAMSON

My darling Lyla,

How I long to be back in England. How I long to see you face to face. There will be so much to say one day. I collect and save the things I want to tell you, the little things to ease you on your way, gentle breezes to launch the fragile craft that is a child setting forth into the world. I hoard these things like marbles in a chest, to pass on to you one day.

Growing up is a confusing, drawn-out thing, and sometimes the places where there are the most people can be the loneliest, and of those crowded lonely places, schools are undoubtedly the worst. But do not be tempted to rush things. Wait and choose a friend, one true friend. Choose her slowly and carefully. Life is a long game, Lyla – the friends that last are the ones that answer to something in yourself, and the friends that last are the only ones that matter.

Here in the Middle East, we British fight the Germans and Italians alone. Things are dangerous and uncertain and I am to go off alone and undercover into the enemy-occupied territory in the north.

By God it is hot here, sand and flies and scorpions. How I long for green grass and deep rivers, for England and to see you, Lyla.

I pray, every morning and every night, that I will one day see you again.

Yours always,

Father

56

CURRICULUM

The summer holidays came to an end, leaves began to brown and redden and drop. The Upper VIth had left: some to marry, some to join the WRAAF and some to do secretarial training. And Lyla had moved up another year. Pinnacle, however, the girls were told, was to remain in London for the foreseeable future. The death of her son and the loss of the school had been a fierce double blow. Aunt Ada was to remain, by what she said was the unanimous vote of the governors, in charge of Garden Hill School for Girls, and was thus at liberty to make all the adjustments she could dream of to the curriculum.

First aid was to be instructed by Miss Macnair as a matter of urgency in case any wounded soldier in need of resuscitation should find himself in the vicinity.

Dreaming, rhetoric, invention, imagination, curiosity and history backwards classes were to be continued, and Currants would soon start – though the content of a Currants class was still as yet entirely a matter of conjecture.

New prefects were appointed and, as far as Lyla could see, they soon became intolerably pleased with themselves, just like the prefects that had gone before. Lyla and Cat were now in the Lower Vth with Primrose as form teacher. Cat saw less of Imelda, and that, from Lyla's point of view, was very satisfactory, though Faye, who no longer had Mary Masters around to chum up with, recruited Imelda as her sidekick.

The winter that came was fierce and bitter. In November the inkwells and water pitchers froze once more. Icicles hung from the goalposts, and all the park was white and sparkling. The lake had frozen solid, and one morning, as a group of girls tumbled through the Orangery in a rush with their skates, Lyla, sitting alone at her easel and watching them, overheard Faye say to Imelda, 'See, she still doesn't have skates. I told you nobody bothers with her.'

'You can borrow mine,' whispered Cat to her.

'But it's you I want to skate with, not anyone else,' answered Lyla.

Cat thought for a minute. 'In that case, I'm going to get myself a fever and get off games and stay inside with you tomorrow, so at least we can be together.'

Lyla was deeply moved by that and grinned at Cat. 'Shall we go up to my room later and see Bucket? *Do* come.'

Cat answered that there was someone she had to

talk to about something before she did that but she might come up later, and Lyla – so chuffed still that Cat would stay in with her the next day – thought no more about who and what that someone and something might be.

57

IN VIOLET'S QUARTERS

Cat did engineer herself a fever by the simple means of dunking Macnair's thermometer in a scalding-hot cup of tea. Miss Macnair, for once, let this wily subterfuge pass. You were supposed to do silent reading if you were off games, but Lyla and Cat decided to spend the afternoon with Violet instead.

Lyla, though touched that Cat should want to spend the afternoon with her instead of skating, was also tormented by the laughter that came from the frozen lake. She crept to the window and, after stroking Violet's ears and whispering to her, wiped away a patch of fug and stood watching the pirouetting and twirling going on below.

'My father knows your father a bit, I've discovered,' Cat remarked, out of the blue.

Lyla tensed. 'Mop says if you come out of a certain sort of hat box and then go to a certain sort of school, then you all end up in the same Gentleman's Club and *everyone* knows *everyone else*. And, actually, that's all rather useful because that means everyone we don't like is generally in the same club and we know not to go there.' Lyla knew she'd been hurtful but couldn't stop herself.

Goaded into having a dig herself, Cat replied, 'Anyway, that's why Father told me to be nice to you.'

'He *told* you to be nice to me?'

'Mmm hmm.' Cat picked up her book.

'Is that the only reason you're my friend?' demanded Lyla.

'Mmm hmm, *obviously* it is.' Cat smiled, and turned away, opening her book.

At that moment, Ada strode in then drew up suddenly, apparently astonished to find Lyla and Cat inside of an afternoon when Fresh Air was The Thing, until she appeared to recollect why she'd come.

'What are you waiting for, girls? Chop-chop,' she said, gesturing vaguely. 'Solomon's waiting on the drive – the pony'll get cold if you don't hurry. Sponge cake and hot chocolate in Ladywood.' She turned to the door, paused and then added in an offhand manner, 'Oh, yes, and there's a lady in Evanses expecting you, Lyla. Something or other for you to try on. I'm told you lack the right footwear for ice?'

Thrilled, Lyla nodded.

'Good, good, well, hurry up. Take the back drive

and get back before they finish skating, or Pigeon'll be after you.'

Huddled together under a blanket, the conversation in the library forgotten, the trap took them out along the drive and past the tiny church at Heaven's Gate where they waved at Father Scott.

'The Rector Scott Talks Rot,' Cat whispered.

Lyla giggled and looked down at the sweet spires and hollows of Ladywood, thinking how they'd soon be sauntering up the cobbled main street to Evanses to buy skates, and how then they'd go and sit by the log fire in Farthings Tea Rooms and drink hot chocolate and eat sponge cake.

'I know!' said Cat suddenly, taking Lyla's hand. 'Let's go tonight! Let's skate by moonlight – wouldn't that be just the thing?'

That night, Lyla and Cat crept from their rooms, met by Sir Galahad, tiptoed down the Great Stairs and went out towards the lake. Stepping outside, they caught their breath – for the thrill of the thing, for the cold and the fear, for the moon that was full and the sky that was high and starry.

The grounds were radiant with ghostly brilliance, every blade and twig encased in glittering glass. A branch snapped eerily under the weight of snow, and an owl hooted as they staggered past it out on to the lake, glassy and freckled with the reflection of stars.

They began with circles, faster and faster, performed figures of eight, spun and turned, twirled and swizzled, transported by the trembling thrill of the speed, the shiver of fear and the cold brilliance of the night.

58

THE WIRELESS

'Hurry, Lyla – it is most important.'

Lyla eyed the envelope Ada held, but as she rose from her desk, Ada tucked it quickly into a pocket and hauled Lyla downstairs to the kitchens. She settled herself on the stool by the enormous Primus stove, very erect, and waited, hands folded on her lap.

Disconcerted by this second appearance of the mistress of the house in her own kitchen, an alarmed Prudence grew giddy and began to drop things. When she sent a second copper pan clattering to the floor, Great Aunt Ada sighed and eyed the clock.

'Well, turn it on,' she snapped.

'Turn what on?' asked Prudence.

'The wireless, of course.' Aunt Ada gestured impatiently at it.

Prudence, in her fluster, had for the first time forgotten the news bulletin at eight, but she hurried over to the wireless and turned it on and they heard that the Allies had halted the Axis advance on Cairo and Suez.

Churchill spoke: '*Now this is not the end. It is not even the beginning of the end, but it is, perhaps, the end of the beginning.*'

Ada rose from her stool, triumphant, victorious and suddenly weightless, as if great anxiety had been lifted from her mind. She skipped about as the words of the Prime Minister resonated around the kitchen.

'*Here we are, and here we stand, a veritable rock of salvation in this drifting world.*'

Ada took Lyla's hands. 'Don't you see – it's marvellous, marvellous, what's happening in Egypt.' She looked into Lyla's eyes. 'This is most important to us both – most important.'

Lyla stared at her light-and-skipping-maiden-great-aunt, and wondered why she should care so much what happened in Egypt.

'Solomon, Solomon!' called Ada. 'D'you hear? We're a rock of salvation in this drifting world. Take the contraption upstairs, it is the end of the beginning or the beginning of the end – I forget which – take it upstairs, I said.'

As the wireless, borne aloft on Solomon's salver, processed out of the kitchen, Prudence's face wobbled and grew pinker, and Lyla thought she might cry, but Ada went to her and said, 'Dear Prudence, you and I will *share* the contraption. D'you see? I've come round to this particular Convenience of the Modern Age. Both as a scientist and as a civilian, I approve of it. I must be kept informed – critical events – victories, and so on – I'll need it every evening at eight.'

That was the beginning of Currants. Currants, as it turned out, were actually *current affairs*, and it appeared now that they had been delayed until current affairs finally began to conform to Great Aunt Ada's worldview and therefore became both palatable to her and a suitable subject for the curriculum of Garden Hill Girls.

Currants began every evening at ten to eight, when Cedric would appear with the logs, and the girls would file down in their nightdresses and several layers of jerseys, and Aunt Ada would be waiting in her smoking jacket and embroidered slippers, and then, finally, Solomon would make an entrance with the ceremonial salver on which stood the newly favourable Contraption of the Modern Age.

The news would start, and the girls would strain to understand it all due to Aunt Ada's interruptions and expostulations, all invariably directed at all the other peoples of Europe who were 'not dependable'.

'Why? Why? Why should we care about Belgium? Well, speak up! What do you care about? Well, what is it? What is it we're fighting for?'

'For the French?' suggested Imelda.

'No! For democracy! For freedom!' Ada glared at the assembled faces.

So it was that a generation of Garden Hill girls came to understand that 'currants' and 'history backwards' were almost the same thing, because actually all the interesting things were happening now. And of course there was no point doing *history forwards* as that meant starting at the beginning of everything, and why would you ever do that unless you were a) in your cradle, or b) in your dotage and thus incapable of comprehending anything other than nonsense concerning burnt bread and round tables, so there was no point, no point at all, to history forwards.

59

A DOUGLAS HAVOC
IN THE DAMSON

My darling Lyla,

*I am a prisoner of war, Lyla, held in a jail at Hasufa,
a scrap of North Africa that still remains in German
hands.*

*The war in Egypt was a very different war to that in
the trenches of Europe. There were no civilians mixed
up in the fighting there, it was a good clean game,
we had a go at them, they had a go at us, then one
of us retreated. Montgomery was a fine commander
and Rommel a fine enemy, and both sides treat their
prisoners fairly.*

*We have one square yard of concrete floor per man, a
wall of barbed wire six feet wide. We dream of food,
of Red Cross parcels and of England. All I have are
the clothes I wore when I was captured taking water
from a well.*

Anything could happen now – the Germans are being beaten back, but we do not know what they will do with us nor where we will end up. Perhaps they will take us with them as they go to Germany or Italy.

How I miss you, for you are all that keeps me going. Men die like flies among us from hunger and disease. We pounce on parcels sent from home like savages and fight among ourselves for scraps of food.

How is dear Ada? She's as wise a person as you'll ever meet, with more wisdom in her head and more tenderness in her than you'll find anywhere. I heard from Solomon a while ago. He worries she is growing frail, some weakness in the heart perhaps, he thinks, though he says she hides it well and soldiers on. I hear that Cedric has laid the ballroom floor with turf for Violet's pasture and that her sleeping quarters are hung with a maharajah's silks. How splendid. Only at Furlongs.

Oh, I would that I were there.

Yours always,

Father

60

RIVERS AND BLACKBERRIES

On the grounds that French was unnecessary, poor Frou-Frou had been relegated by Ada to being in charge of the stationery cupboard, but there was now such a shortage of paper and pens in the country that the stationery cupboard was empty and Frou-Frou no longer had a role to play until a thing called wool-gathering was begun.

Wool-gathering, the most miserable of all Great Aunt Ada's initiatives, involved the disentangling of filthy-smelling wool from barbed wire and barbed trees such as thorns in order to send it on to the manufacturers of soldiers' uniforms, being, as they were, in dire need of more wool.

Not surprisingly, Frou-Frou soon handed in her notice, and Great Aunt Ada declared herself victorious for she had had, from the start, great scorn for Frou-Frou.

A new initiative was suddenly announced: knitting. Instead of wool-gathering there would now be knitting.

In the afternoons, the girls would gather around the fire in the Painted Hall, Primrose would read Shakespeare aloud, and the girls were to knit for prisoners, because something had made Ada all of a sudden most agitated about the well-being of British prisoners in far-flung places. The girls must do all they could for British prisoners of war, must give their utmost and so forth. Even Aunt Ada herself took to knitting and went at it with fearsome vigour at all hours, going about the corridors trailing reams of coarse and rather smelly wool, which, as she proudly explained, were kindly donated to the nation by her own sheep.

The haws ripened and the apples reddened, and Tawny began once more to chop logs and burn leaves. There was to be no more lacrosse, no, no, every girl at Furlongs would pull her weight, give her all in this hour of need. Pigeon was to supervise the girls as they collected acorns for the nation's pigs, because the nation's pigs had not enough to eat. On blustery afternoons Lyla and Cat would find Tawny and linger by his fire or they might roam far through the woods, talking and talking, but still there were the things that Lyla couldn't voice.

Christmas came and went, and still the girls and Ada knitted. Gradually the days grew longer. Spring came and the days grew still longer and hotter, until, finally, Aunt Ada announced that she had 'temporarily abolished education'. No, no, during the summer the girls must read. Everything they needed to prepare themselves for life was in novels, plays and poetry. Dickens, Shakespeare, Tolstoy. The writers, didn't everyone see, were the rule-breakers, the people who changed things, the people who built the ladders to the places you wanted to be. Yes, during the day the girls must take books, they must go outside and they must read – and they would find that each book would be a stepping stone to somewhere else. Prudence was to provide picnic lunches, and each girl was to choose a book from Ada's library.

On such a day in August, Cat, Lyla, Flea and Elspeth sat with their books and their picnics at the boundary of the park amidst bracken and foxgloves and ate their ration of bread and cheese and lolled about in the sun, flicking off the summer flies and talking of the things they'd read, the things they dreamed of doing one day. Lyla was happy for a while. But then Imelda joined them and said, 'I want to be just like my mother.'

'I do too,' said Flea.

Lyla shrugged as if to shake a thing away, and she decided that life was easy if you had no imagination, because then you couldn't imagine any other way of being than what you knew.

Imelda turned to Lyla. 'What about you, Lyla – do you want a life like your mother's?'

Lyla rolled over on to her side, plucked irritably at the turf and said nothing. She knew Imelda was only jealous that she'd been supplanted in Cat's affections by Lyla.

'None of us will have lives like our parents,' Cat interjected breezily. 'Primrose says it will be a very different world when the war is over . . .'

The sun had grown hotter. A horsefly settled on Lyla's leg and, scowling, she flicked it away. After a while, she reached out for her lunch bag, rose and meandered away as if there were nothing wrong and she had simply decided to go in search of blackberries. She lingered a little by a rowan to give Cat the opportunity to join her.

'Are you all right?' asked Cat.

'Of course I am.'

Lyla glanced back and saw how Imelda was watching them there together beneath the rowan, and turned a sunny, breezy face to Cat and said, 'Tawny told me there's a sheep track through the bracken. It's near here and it takes you to a place called Shearwater where there's a deep pool you can swim in and a boathouse. Let's go there.'

They splashed in water that held sunlight down to its bottom and then lazed about on the turf, their hair gleaming and twisted, their faces turned to the sun, and they stayed there dozing.

'Robin's happier, now you know,' Cat said. 'Listen,

he says –' she fumbled about in the pocket of the dress strewn on the grass beside her – '"*I have a really good friend now, called Jack. Jack likes playing Racing Demon too and we are in the same dorm this term, so that's really good.*"'

Lyla, still jealous of Cat having a brother to write letters to her as well as a mother who wrote every week, remained silent.

'Mother says she might come down one day,' said Cat, lying back and closing her eyes. 'She says she's been saving petrol coupons and the hospital might give her a week off in July. If they do and she comes down, I know she'd love to meet you.'

'Oh, Mop really wants to meet you too,' said Lyla. She fumbled for the pocket of her dress and pulled out a letter. 'Mop's awfully busy too with all the things she does, but she wants to come down and visit too.'

Cat rolled back on to her side, opened her eyes and looked at Lyla, who began to read.

'*My darling Lyla,*

I'm so busy just now with War Work and making jams and parachutes and probably I am going to be a nurse and an ambulance driver. I'm in such a rush just now, due to all the KNITTING I have to do because of the soldiers being cold and needing jerseys and socks.'

Cat sat up. 'She's awfully busy, isn't she? How will she do jams and parachutes and knitting as well as driving ambulances and nursing soldiers?'

Lyla turned a little away from her friend, as if the sun was bothering her. Holding the letter a little closer to her chest and shielding it from view with her hands, she read on:

> '*It is FOREVER since I saw you and I do so want to meet all the friends you are making and hear about all the fun you are having and I don't mind at all about marks for things like mathematics or grammar.*
>
> *I am making lots of plans for all the things we will do and all the lovely islands we can go to when the war is over and we are together again.*
>
> *I do miss you and wish you weren't so far away.*
>
> *All my love,*
>
> *Mother*'

Cat was silent. She watched Lyla fold the letter and tuck it deeply into the pocket of her dress, and after a while said, gently, 'They always come on Tuesdays, don't they, her letters?'

'Oh yes,' answered Lyla. 'She writes every week, just like yours does.'

Cat, still watching Lyla, paused for a while, then said, 'Come on. It's getting cold. Let's go.'

They dressed in silence, and as they walked back across the park, Cat took Lyla's hand and held it tightly.

THE RED CROSS

In the dark, huddled months, the house filled once more with an arctic chill and everything froze, even, once again, the ink pots. Primrose, most upset, showed Ada a hot-water bottle that had actually frozen solid overnight. The girls slept in all the clothing they could lay their hands on and went about wrapped in blankets and eiderdowns. In the evenings, everyone would gather for warmth, and for light, in the Painted Hall which, having only one window, could actually be blacked out, all the other windows of Great Aunt Ada's house being too large to be covered effectively.

One such evening, Great Aunt Ada erupted into the room, waving *The Times* about.

'Their diets are deficient, of course; their rooms damp; they're fed only cabbage and barley . . . We must do something – it is most urgent.'

The girls turned to her, baffled and amused, for Great Aunt Ada pitched herself with relentless vim and vigour from one mission to the next, and no one had any idea at all who it was that was only eating barley and cabbage.

'The Red Cross must have parcels for our men.' She glared at the room. 'Do you know how many of our own soldiers are held captive? Well, do you?'

Of course no one did, not even the Red Cross, nor of course Great Aunt Ada, though she was above admitting such things. Lyla and Cat glanced at each other, grinning and rolling their eyes.

'Great Aunt Ada Modern Crusader,' whispered Cat. But Lyla, watching her great aunt, was wondering if there was perhaps some method to her madness, for sometimes she seemed very daft, sometimes very shrewd.

'They need sustenance, yes . . . processed cheese is the thing, herrings, sardines, condensed milk, dried eggs, a meat roll, a tin of creamed rice, perhaps a bar or two of soap. It's all most imperative.'

She glared at the room again,

'The Geneva Convention, girls – it's all in the Geneva Convention, hmm? Our men must have letters, they must have parcels, and they must be sent food and clothing, and so on.'

British prisoners of war were still much on Ada's mind that year, and this new craze of hers, which came to be known as 'Prisoners', was pressed with the utmost urgency upon both girls and staff.

So it was that after *Wool-gathering* came *Prisoners*, and Tawny was put to heaving crates of bootlaces, tinned puddings and such like into the hall every evening ready for the girls to make up the boxes.

62

CHRISTMAS

That year, the Painted Hall was out of bounds on the day before Christmas Eve, admittance granted only to Solomon and Tawny. There was to be a concert; the villagers were to come. Everyone needed cheering up, their morale boosting and so forth.

That evening the girls took their places on the staircase, smallest at the bottom, biggest at the top, to stand and gaze at the Painted Hall as it flickered with fire and candlelight, every shield, axe and antler festooned with garlands of ivy and holly.

Solomon opened the main door and the children from the village poured in to be presented with the spectacle of three hundred Garden Hill girls dressed in cloaks and scarves and mittens, earnestly singing 'It Came Upon a Midnight Clear', and they gawped at the splendour and scale of it all.

There was a sumptuous buffet with rabbit and duck, and even what Cat called the whiskery-bosom-to-belly staff like Threadgold and Trumpet had painted lips and frothy hair, and Prudence ascended from the kitchens in her flowered overall and tin hat, and Solomon allowed himself to relax for a minute or two and smile.

At the end of the evening, the girls arranged themselves like a ladder up the stairs and sang the school anthem:

We look to the future, to what lies ahead,
We look to a life full of work and of cheer,
To a life free of spite, free of malice and fear.
We stand all together and we'll always be true
To the friendships we make, to the hopes
That we hope and we ask,
Am I gentle and brave? Am I bold? Am I strong?
Do I have courage and kindness and truth
As I stand hand in hand with the friends of my youth?

The Rector Scott Talks Rot said a prayer for all those who were far from home, for those who had brothers or fathers at the Front, and for Cedric Tawny, whose two sons were serving in France. Each child from Ladywood was given a knitted stocking, and they hurried out, shaking their heads in bemusement at the soap and the walnuts that were in it, and at the many oddities of the inside of a large English country house.

63

JAMES AND JOHN TAWNY

The New Year began, and everything was much as before: there was still cauliflower cheese for lunch and Welsh rarebit for dinner; Faye still came top in everything; Elspeth still had chillblains and came bottom in everything; and Lyla still went up and down the stairs with Violet's various buckets.

In early February, Aunt Ada stood at the top of the Great Stairs and announced the prayers and, bowing her head deeply, asked the girls to remember James and John Tawny, the sons of Cedric Tawny, both now dead. They were to have farmed this land one day as their father had, and their father's father had – two brave sons, his only children, lost to Cedric forever.

The snowdrops came once more, but it had been a bleak start to a year that grew bleaker.

Aunt Ada was very distracted throughout January and February. She was devoted to the wireless news bulletins and what was happening in Africa, and she kept mislaying Little Gibson's cuttlebone, which upset the canary a great deal.

Lyla worried about Ada, who'd grown increasingly jumpy and preoccupied for no reason that Lyla could understand. She'd lost interest in her Pink Dandelions, there being no longer any imminent threat from Germans in the Bristol Channel. It was only 'Prisoners' that appeared to still be a matter of urgency.

'Come on, Lyla,' Cat would say of an evening. 'Prisoners.'

Lyla would drag her heels a little, bored as she was with packing boxes of bootlaces and tinned Ambrosia for the soldiers that might be in foreign jails.

'No, Lyla, it's important,' Cat would say, gazing at her friend.

And so Lyla would spend evening after evening sealing and addressing boxes, because Cat thought that, *you never knew, they might just be desperately needed by someone somewhere.*

After the snowdrops, and entirely in accordance with Ada's pattern, came the bluebells and the primroses.

Lyla walked with Cat one afternoon through the Orangery to go and fetch boots and coats. Cat pointed. Someone, perhaps one of the more daring sixth-formers, had placed her bra on the upper part of Hermes, but neither Cat nor Lyla giggled, for the year so far had a gloom that couldn't be shifted.

Wrapping their coats tightly about themselves,

they went out into the old knot garden. The roses had long been uprooted and replaced with vegetables. Cat paused, looked up and –as if it had only just occurred to her because of the tree being right there – said, 'It's a long time since you gave me a letter from your father.'

Lyla never thought about her father's letters at all. She would simply hand them to Cat without a second thought, and Cat would give them to Solomon.

Cat waited under the tree and Lyla called back to her, 'Come on, it's cold.'

In the potting shed, as they collected a sack of what Mr Tawny called 'earlies', which were actually just a kind of potato that grew earlier than the other ones, Cat asked, 'Don't you ever think about him?'

'Who?' asked Lyla, though she knew exactly who Cat meant and, in truth, the deaths of Brenda's father and of Cedric's sons had combined to inch the undercurrent of her thoughts in Father's direction. 'Never,' she said.

Cat's forehead creased a little as she looked at Lyla. They were silent for a long while, bending side by side, dropping the earlies into a furrow. As they washed their hands under the icy tap beside the potting shed, Cat asked, 'You know, you might be able to visit your mother one day – Primrose lets girls do that sometimes, if, say, your second cousin or someone like that has something happen to him. I am sure Primrose would let you if you asked her.'

'I might . . .' answered Lyla, instantly dismissing the idea, for she knew, deep down, she'd never go to London.

Lyla could no longer think about Mop with any clarity, nor even for any great length of time, for if she did she would grow uneasy. A dim awareness that there were things she did not wish to acknowledge stopped her from looking further or deeper. There were things half known, things half remembered, half seen, that had, perhaps because of the deaths of Cedric's sons, begun to waken, to stir and scuffle in her mind like jackdaws in a chimney. Lyla, who felt as fragile as a porcelain thing that might crack and shatter under the faintest of pressure, knew also that these were things she mustn't allow into the light, things she must keep down like rats in a cellar.

She glanced at Cat and frowned, wondering why her friend was suggesting she visit Mop now when she'd never suggested it before, then took a deep breath and said brightly, 'Oh, by the way, I'm going to read you my letter from Mop this evening. It came today because her letters don't always come on Tuesdays any more.'

Cat smiled gently. 'You're so similar, you and your mother,' she began carefully. 'Sometimes it's like hearing you talk when you read her letters.'

64

THE GENEVA CONVENTION

A new sign had suddenly appeared on the door to the Billiard Room.

TOP SECRET
NO ENTRY TO PREFECTS
PETTY OFFICIALS OF ANY STRIPE
NOR TO ANYONE WITHOUT PERMISSION

That night at Prisoners, Ada declared with her customary vigour that British prisoners of war were not so much hungry as *bored*. Their spirits must be kept up. They must have board games. Board games were the thing for raising morale, whiling away the hours, encouraging them, and so on.

The girls would fill the boxes for prisoners with processed cheese, tinned puddings and so forth in the Painted Hall as usual, but before they were sealed, they were to be wheeled in a wicker log basket to the door of the Billiard Room to have the board game added by Ada herself, and in this Ada must be helped by Lyla Spence.

'Why do I have to do it?' Lyla complained to Cat later.

'Of course you do. I would if I were you,' answered Cat quietly.

'Well, you're not,' said Lyla.

'If I help you will you do it?' asked Cat.

And so it was that both Lyla and Cat presented themselves in the Billiard Room, and when Solomon with his customary flourish and sense of occasion opened the door to them, Lyla saw that it was much changed, for the gelignite, blasting powder, ammonite and all the other ingredients that went into Pink Dandelions had been swept aside into a far corner, and stacked around the edges of the room were now piles and piles of wooden boxes with the word 'MONOPOLY' running across the side in black. At the far end of the room there was a separate table on which were lined up lots of lines of silver top hats, several piles of small folded papers and a screwdriver.

'Yes, yes, Monopoly! A game manufactured by Waddingtons, who have kindly donated some to our own prisoners of war. It is a most amusing game, great fun and just the thing for when you're bored and locked in a jail and far from home. Now, d'you see, you are to take a Monopoly set, like so, and pass it to me –' she gestured to the table with the screwdriver –

'and I will . . . well, I will check it is complete, mend anything broken and so on, and then I will pass it back to you, like pass the parcel, d'you see? And you will then add it to a box, then seal the box and address it to the International Red Cross Committee in Geneva.'

'We could give them some other games too,' suggested Lyla. 'I think Conflict is quite a good game—'

Great Aunt Ada looked astonished at such a notion. 'No no, the kind of game that English men like to play when in prison, the only game worth its salt, d'you know, is Monopoly.'

'Yes,' Cat agreed. 'They want to play Monopoly, Lyla.'

Those evenings in the Billiard Room were wonderful. There, with the large fire burning and in the company of those who loved her, Lyla felt safe and happy and didn't really mind at all about only being able to put Monopoly in the boxes rather than any other game.

Ada would work away most intently and Lyla would wink at Cat and roll her eyes, for Aunt Ada appeared so very earnest about the game, checking and double-checking all the various pieces of each set – the little metal hats and dice and so on – until finally she would replace the lid and pass it over to the billiard table and urge them to hurry their sealing and labelling, and again Lyla would smile and roll her eyes, most amused by Ada's peculiar view on what was required by an Englishman in captivity.

'Not to worry, not to worry,' Ada would say, a little impatiently, as Lyla double-checked the list of contents. 'Don't you see, it's the *game* that will keep them going, not the cheese and so on.'

'Don't you see, she *is* dotty. I said she was, and she *is*,' whispered Lyla. 'I've never heard of anyone sending Monopoly to prisoners. I mean, it's just a game. It's not as though it could feed you or keep you warm. Anyway, there might be other games they prefer.'

'Well, she wouldn't be doing it for no reason at all,' answered Cat quietly.

65

A SHORT-WAVE S 88/5
ABWEHR TRANSMITTER

Rather abruptly in April that year, Great Aunt Ada banished *The Times* from Furlongs. The Wireless was coming in very handy indeed: it carried no nonsense or tittle-tattle, nor news that wasn't news. So, from now on, no printed press was to cross the threshold of her house. As in all things, Great Aunt Ada was thorough about the whole business.

At the end of that term Primrose announced that both the Art Cup and the Art Scholarship this year would go to Lyla Spence. Lyla, who'd never in all her life won an award, went to the top of the Great Stairs and took the cup. She heard the applause and her eyes filled with tears for the longing that she had to tell her mother that she, Lyla, her mother's daughter, had won a scholarship for art.

Lyla walked back from church with Elspeth that Sunday and listened to Elspeth talking about all the things she would write about to her mother that week. Lyla had less and less heart for letter-writing. Each week she found she had less and less to say, and each week she was increasingly uneasy about the letters she wrote.

Making her way upstairs to put away her gloves and cloak, two fourth-formers passed Lyla, and as they did, they flattened themselves against the wall as if to put some distance between themselves and her. One nudged the other, tugged her hand and whispered, 'That's her,' and they carried on down the stairs, still whispering. *What was the matter with them?* Lyla thought scornfully. She sighed and then, remembering how Bucket – not being allowed in sacred places like churches – was alone upstairs, she hurried a little. Further up, she passed more fourth-formers, who did the same as the others. Lyla stopped and stared after them, wondering what on earth was going on.

On the landing, at a hushed sort of whispering from the North Gallery, she paused by Sir Galahad and strained to listen, but could make nothing out, so she continued down the corridor. At the door of the Yellow Silk Room, she saw a clutch of girls watching her. They caught Lyla's eye and backed away, whispering among themselves.

Puzzled, Lyla turned away to enter the room, and then stopped abruptly. Her throat constricted and her stomach lurched: pinned to the door was a newspaper cutting with a large photograph of Mop on it. A big red crayon circle had been hand-drawn around the caption below the picture: Mop's name, *Florence Spence*. Terrified, Lyla stared at Mop's image: the mother whose face she'd not seen for three long years. As she stared, she grew confused, for nothing about Mop's happy, sparkling eyes and smile conformed to the anxious, lonely image Lyla had so fiercely nurtured.

Lyla's eyes moved to the heading of the article.

THE HON. FLORENCE SPENCE, SOCIETY DIVORCEE, DISCOVERED WITH GERMAN SPY

Lyla put a hand to the wall to support herself.

She snatched the cutting from the door, tearing the corner of it, and went into her room, walking very slowly across to the stool at the foot of her bed, where she sat herself down. Bewildered, Lyla read the heading again and then one more time. *DISCOVERED WITH GERMAN SPY. What did it mean? It couldn't be right. It couldn't be true.* The cutting trembled like a leaf in her hands as she tried to make sense of what she read.

A short-wave German S88/5 Abwehr transmitter was found on Mr Heinrich Meier when he was apprehended late last night in the company of Florence Spence at an address in London. Large

amounts of cash were found on Meier, who has been
in this country for a number of months posing as an
English gentleman under the name of Henry Mayer.
He is reported to have been moving around Britain
for some months in the company of Florence Spence
and to have been reporting on British troop positions
and movements. Florence Spence claims to have been
unaware of these activities. Heinrich Meier will be
executed next week at Pentonville Prison.

Lyla, still struggling to make some sense of it, read it once more. *Mop with a German spy? No, no, Mop was at home. She was at Lisson Square. She'd be painting, and Winnie would be there, and there'd be tulips on the table, and . . . It was wrong, the newspaper people had made a mistake.*

She clenched her fist, scrumpling the paper into a ball. *Who'd done this? Who'd put it in her room?* She flung it across the room. A chill ran through her – *Who else had seen it? Had every Garden Hill girl seen it?* She ran to the door, flung it open and raced along the corridor to the South Gallery. There she found a cluster of girls in front of the washstand and the same newspaper cutting pasted over the glass, with the same hand-drawn red circle around the name 'Florence Spence'. Lyla paused, then elbowed her way through the crowd, reached the washstand and yanked the newspaper cutting off the glass.

'IT'S NOT TRUE!' she screamed at them. Then she went pelting along the North Corridor, shoving girls aside as she went, and into the Chinese Room, and then into the North Gallery – and in each dormitory she found the same front page of *The Times* with Mop's face splashed across it.

She ran blindly back to her room and hurled herself face down on to the bed.

'Lyla—'

'Go away, Cat.' Lyla beat her legs in grief against the mattress.

Cat was still there.

Lyla didn't want to see anyone again. Ever. Cat waited a good long while. When the heaving of Lyla's chest and the thrashing of her legs subsided, she approached Lyla's bed and said quietly, 'Lyla, I think it was Faye that did it. You didn't see her in church, did you?'

Lyla paused, then shook her head.

'No, I didn't either . . .' Cat paused. 'You know, Father told me she wanted that art scholarship. He told me her father's been making a bit of a nuisance of himself, you know – you see, they're both governors.'

'I don't care about Faye or governors or—' Lyla buried her head deep into the pillow again and screamed into it. 'I don't CARE what the papers say – none of it's true. None of it!'

Cat tried to stroke Lyla's hair, but Lyla batted her hand away and said, 'Not one word of it is true.'

'Even if it *is* true . . .' Cat began slowly and cautiously. 'Even if they are right, she would never have known who he was or what he was doing – she was probably just lonely—'

'Lonely . . . ?' Lyla turned on her friend like a wild thing, and then added in a savage, soul-wrenching screech, 'She didn't have to be lonely . . . She could've been with me.'

After a long while, Lyla grew quieter, calmer. She turned to Cat, her eyes wide, almost imploring her friend to believe what she was about to say. 'We used to have fun. Mother and I used to have fun.'

'Did you, Lyla? Did you *really*?'

Lyla, tear-stained and swollen with shame and hurt, retorted, 'Yes, and anyway, I'm not staying here. I can't stay here. *Everyone* will know.' She bent her head. 'It will be just like when Father divorced Mother and all the world knew because of the newspapers. All over again.'

66

SIREN

Cat had to leave, and Lyla stayed for the rest of that day alone in her room, her door locked against the world, her feelings lurching from towering rage at Faye, to scorn at newspapermen who didn't know anything about anything, to fear for Mop, until she grew weak and febrile. Towards eleven that night, the childishness in her came to the fore and she set out to make trouble.

She didn't care about anyone or anything, and she would let the world know that was the case.

Barefoot and in her nightdress, Lyla crept along the corridor. She passed the Staffroom and paused, hearing the murmuring from within, and smelling Primrose's evening cigarette. She passed the dormitories in the East Wing and stopped outside, thinking angrily of Faye Peak, who was sure to be in there.

Her eyes narrowed and her fists clenched.

They're all cruel and horrid and they don't know anything about anything.

Lyla stomped onwards not knowing where she was going nor what she would do. She arrived at the narrow stairs that led to the Attic and climbed up them, thinking to hide herself away up there forever. At the top of the stairs she saw the stars that shone through the open door to the rooftop and they drew her on and up.

The stars were cold and high, the late frost already freckling the stone. She climbed on to the parapet and walked along it between the statues, looking down.

Nothing matters. Nothing matters any more. I hate it all. I hate them all.

She gazed through glimmering eyes at the stars and, as she did so, she lost her footing on a piece of stone worked loose by frost over the years, and slipped. Wincing with pain, she tried to rise, clutching at the wall of the parapet to pull herself up. Her fingers fumbled and found something cold and metallic, and as she clutched at it to haul herself to her feet, she realized that it was the air-raid siren that was bolted to the stone.

With sudden violent anger, she clutched its handle, turned it and heard, through her tears, its slow, eerie wail. Her anger fuelled her arm and she cranked the handle and her eyes watched the radial veins of the siren spin till they became a hypnotic blur. She drove the thing to its maximum pitch and kept it there, the sound rising and rising, suffocating the pain in her heart, the banshee cry haunting the rooftops and towers with a tidal swelling. She let it roll back before cranking it up with redoubled force, filling the air with a spine-chilling drone that rose and fell, rose and fell, like waves on a shore.

Terrified sheep skittered from one end of the park to the other, like drifts of snow in a storm. Cedric Tawny was running from his cottage and Mabel Rawle was on her new motorbike and all the Home Guard appeared on bicycles, all risen from their beds and converging on Furlongs.

As Lyla witnessed all this unfold, her hands began to tremble and her anger to wane and she collapsed to the ground, crying and shaking, and she remained there for some time, huddled against the parapet.

It was Great Aunt Ada who found her and hauled her to her feet.

'Good men and women hauled from their beds?' she said grimly. 'Nothing that happens to you in life can ever justify you causing fear to others. You must not think only of yourself. You'll apologize to Cedric Tawny and Mabel Rawle, to the Home Guard and to the girls and the staff for the fear you've caused, child.'

'I'm not a child.'

Great Aunt Ada bent to Lyla and said, more gently now, 'You have *behaved* like a child, Lyla. Don't you see you have frightened people, really frightened them?'

Lyla turned from Ada and, clawing at the stone wall, sobbed, 'I hate everyone. Everyone and everything. There's no point to anything at all. School. Lessons. Knitting. Wool-gathering, Growing up. Boxes for prisoners. What is the point of it all? Why should I bother with any of it?'

'That is something we also all feel at different stages in our lives, Lyla, and, yes, it might well seem for a long time yet that there is no point to anything. The things that have happened to you will be with you forever; I cannot pretend otherwise. Oh, yes, the joy and the pain will stay with you forever –' Ada looked away – 'as bright and searing as if they'd happened yesterday. But in time you will know that the moments that stay with you forever, they are the things that make you what you are: both the moments of bottomless pain and those of unbridled joy. Everything in between will simply fade away.'

Just then the all-clear sounded from below. Ada took Lyla in her arms and held her, and there on the roof of Furlongs, her bare feet on the stone, Lyla heard the single sustained note of the all-clear and as it went on and on something inside her began to unravel. The note went on and on, unwinding the stony walls that circled the scarred centre of her, stripping her almost to her core, and finally, as it died on the wind, she whispered, broken, 'I wish anyone else was my mother – *anyone but her.*'

Ada drew away and said, 'The habit of hiding things from yourself has become second nature to you. But step by step, make yourself look at things hard in the face. When you can admit to yourself the way things are, you will be easier with yourself – the way forward will become clear – d'you see – and straight. Don't turn away from those that love you. Take love where it is given. Mine, Solomon's, Catherine Lively's, Lovell's . . . Oh, my dear, you are so very loved.'

Ada took Lyla's hand.

'In spite of everything, Lyla, in spite of my beloved mare spending an entire war in a first-floor bedroom, in spite of every room of my house being overrun with swarms of schoolgirls, in spite of sirens sounding from my rooftops, you are . . . Look at me, Lyla. Look me in the eyes and listen to my words . . . You are the most entirely perfect great niece an old great aunt could stumble upon, and the most entirely lovable daughter a mother or a father could want.'

67

PEAK

In the morning, Lyla dressed and tidied her room and tucked Bucket into his basket. Then she went to the mirror and looked at her reflection.

'I am what I am. I am what I am. They can take me or leave me,' she said aloud.

Lyla joined the Lower VI girls that filed along the corridor. In front of her was Imelda, who hurried her pace to increase the space between herself and Lyla.

Imelda Pole Suburban Soul.

Lyla lifted her chin and walked down the curling stairs and into the hall. She heard, heard the shifting and shuffling, saw the hostility ripple across the room. The whispering rose, more heads were turning, more fingers pointing. Lyla scanned the room and saw that there was no place for her at all – in the whole hall – no place for her to sit. Ada stood at the lectern, watching. Lyla looked about and still could find no space. Ada rapped her fingers on the lectern, and still no one moved to make room for Lyla. No one wanted her beside them, not a single girl. It was as tribal a closing of ranks as if Lyla had been of a different species. *I have known this before. They can move away from me – they can say what they want, think what they want.*

Lyla's eyes began to blur, but she blinked hard and lifted her head. Somewhere someone was calling to her, but she couldn't see who, and she lowered her head, for now there were tears on her cheeks.

Then she heard someone drag back a chair to stand, and make their way across the hall, and she felt someone take her hand.

Cat.

Cat had kept a place for her. As everyone watched, she led Lyla across the hall and together they sat in the place she'd saved for Lyla and she put her hand on Lyla's knee and smiled at her.

Lyla gave a fleeting, tremulous smile in return, but now that she was finally sitting and her face hidden, she found that she was shaking.

Cat placed her hand over Lyla's trembling fingers.

'She didn't *know* he was a spy,' whispered Lyla.

Great Aunt Ada, a sheaf of papers in her hand, announced the hymn in a most vigorous, uncompromising kind of way. Lyla, watching her warily, prepared herself for the worst.

After the hymn the girls sat. Ada went to the lectern and read a series of announcements, birthdays, a Staff vs. Girls hockey match for Saturday, a Girls vs. Village rounders match for the following week, and so on. Then she told the girls to rise for the school anthem, for the words were most appropriate that day. As she spoke, a motor screeched importantly to a halt on the gravel outside. Ada lifted her head and waited. The front door was opened.

Ada raised her hand. 'Ah Mr . . . Peak, is it?'

'Yes, Faye's father.'

'Do join us, Mr Peak. We were just about to rise for the school anthem.'

The girls, a little surprised, shuffled to their feet.

Primrose played the opening bar and Ada led the singing, in a stirring sort of manner. Mr Peak, pressed against the door, looked about, shifty and increasingly discomfited as the girls sang,

When our lives have been lived
And our dreams have been dreamed,
Memories of this, like the scraps of a song
The sound of our laughter, the sound of our tears
Ripple like pebbles through water, back to our
    childhood
To the games and the goals when together we
    stood.
We will ask, *Did I have courage and kindness and truth*
Was I gentle and brave? Was I bold? Was I strong?
When I stood hand in hand with the friends of my youth?

When the girls sat once more, Peak looked about uncomfortably, for there was no place for him and he was too ungainly a man to sit cross-legged on a stone floor that already had three hundred schoolgirls on it.

'Faye Peak, come here. Stand at the front before your schoolmates, please,' Ada commanded. 'I understand this is your father?'

Faye, reddening a little, gave a faint nod.

'Your father's here because he's concerned about the probity and reputation of the school, as I believe were you. In fact, I believe you were so concerned that you felt it necessary to sneak out of school during school hours and go into Ladywood and purchase, what was it – yes – precisely *eight* copies of *The Times* so that everyone in the entire school should be aware of the unhappy circumstances of the mother of one of your classmates, and you then decided to pin these up around the walls of a house that does not belong to you. Is that so? And you chose all the most public places, did you not, where everyone would pass and see them? Where you knew you would cause most hurt to the classmate in question?'

Faye bowed her head.

'Faye, you are to return to, remind me, is it –' Ada peered at the letter in her hand – 'Hendon . . . yes. I understand your father would like to return you to Hendon, and you wish to go?'

Faye, now crimson and staring at the floor, lowered

her chin further as if to bury her entire head in her chest.

'You may go, Faye, if you fear that some scandal might attach itself to your own good name by remaining here, but I will tell you this, all of you, Faye Peak, Mr Peak, girls . . . You are all unhealthily interested in the news articles regarding Florence Spence.' Her voice grew quieter and yet more vehement. 'So much you all know, but this perhaps you don't: scandal attaches easily to a woman. Oh yes, much more easily than to a man.' She paused and took a deep breath and said, fierce and slow, 'Now, you will – all of you – go out into the world one day and you will make mistakes, and some mistakes will be more public than others because some of us, Faye Peak, are more interesting than others.'

She looked to the back of the hall, where Peak still stood beside his daughter's trunk.

'Peak, take your daughter back to Hendon. You are welcome to her. Faye, you may leave. Those of you who do not wish to leave the school may stand.'

For a moment no one moved. Girls glanced covertly, uncertainly at one another. Then, very slowly, Cat rose to her feet, then Lyla, and for a long moment the two of stood side by side, alone. Then Brenda rose and Flea – then one by one, every girl in the Upper Vth rose, and more were rising, now in clutches of five or six, and they kept on rising till everyone was standing, even Imelda.

68

WORN TO THE BONE

The school resumed its normal rhythms.

The Tuesday following Lyla's night on the roof, she was toasting bread in the Painted Hall and waiting for Cat to join her.

'Tuesday?' said Cat, settling down beside her. Seeing the letter in Lyla's hand, she smiled gently and said, 'No, Lyla, let's play Rummy or Conflict.'

Lyla hesitated, the folded letter still in her hand. She had decided not to read it unless Cat asked her to, because reading the letters to Cat had made her feel more and more uneasy with each passing week. Smiling, she handed Cat a piece of National Loaf and was about to place the letter back in her pocket when she saw Imelda approaching. Imelda had been rudderless since Faye had left, always trying to draw Cat's attention and to insinuate herself into Cat's favour once more.

She held a rolled-up newspaper, which she rapped against her palm as she eyed Lyla and the letter on her lap, and there was something in the hard stare Imelda gave Lyla as she drew closer that put Lyla on guard.

'Well, go on, read it out,' said Imelda.

Lyla tensed. 'Oh, it's not very interesting this week, actually.'

'Go on,' said Imelda, her lips curling a little upwards, her eyes sharp and challenging, still rapping the rolled-up paper against her palm.

Growing uncomfortable, Brenda and Elspeth and Flea picked up their mugs of Bovril and shuffled back a little. Lyla's hand hesitated. Imelda suddenly swooped and lunged at the letter and held it far out so everyone could see.

Cat leaped up to snatch it from Imelda, but Imelda lifted it out of reach.

'She doesn't *have* to read it,' said Cat.

'I'll read it, shall I then? Shall I, Lyla?' taunted Imelda.

Lyla, paralysed with horror, stared at the floor.

'Stop it,' commanded Cat.

'Actually, I think I will,' said Imelda, and began to read aloud:

'*My darling Lyla,*

I hope you are well and not at all upset about the things that are written in newspapers. Newspapers are always wrong about everything and of course I had no idea who Henry Mayer was. I might come and see you next week if I can get the petrol but all the hospitals are very crowded just now, with those poor men in the corridors and on the floors and I'm working day and night and worn to the bone . . .'

Imelda lowered the letter. 'Day and night and worn to the bone,' she repeated scornfully.

Day and night was not right, Lyla was thinking. *Probably nurses did not work day and night.*

Cat lunged again at the letter, but Imelda leaped aside and placed herself between Cat and Lyla and sneered, 'Shall we see what address it says, Lyla?'

'Lisson Square,' said Lyla, for she was certain, on all counts, of that.

'Not, perhaps, America?' taunted Imelda triumphantly, glancing over at Cat, for it appeared she really, really wanted Cat's approval.

'No –' Lyla looked up, confused – 'not America.'

'See, Cat!' said Imelda triumphantly. 'It's all lies! Because I –' Imelda brandished the rolled-up newspaper – 'happen to know she is in America.'

Lyla began to tremble. *What was Imelda saying? Where was Mop? Where was she?*

'Don't Imelda – don't you dare!' said Cat.

A suffocating panic rose in Lyla and she stammered, 'Sh-she's n-not in America . . . she w-wouldn't go there – she wouldn't leave—'

But Imelda interrupted. 'Don't you see, Cat, her mother's not even in *Lisson Square, London NW3* – she's in America. She's in New York—'

'Don't say another word, Imelda.' Cat lunged at Imelda and the newspaper.

Imelda made a break for the door. When she reached it, she turned back to the room and, still holding the letter above her head, announced loudly so all could hear, 'I *do* dare. Because the papers have pictures of her in New York.'

America? Mop in America? Could that be true?

'You see, Cat, you're always sticking up for her, but all she tells you is lies. Every week – every single week – you've sat and listened to her letters, Cat. And every word of them has been a lie – she wrote them herself, every word. Lyla Spence's mother isn't a nurse or an ambulance driver. Don't you see? Lyla writes them on a Sunday – she actually writes a letter to herself and puts it in the out tray and then – guess what – surprise, surprise, every Tuesday she gets a letter, doesn't she?'

Lyla, like a broken thing, stumbled to her feet, her shoulders hunched, her face to the ground, and crept across the room, but Cat was snatching at her sleeve and trying to take her hand.

'I don't mind, Lyla. That is, it doesn't matter—'

Lyla pulled herself free but Cat tugged at her and whispered, 'I've known all along—'

Lyla stopped and turned to Cat. 'What do you mean?'

'Well, not quite all along, but I've known for a long time – I guessed – but I understand – I understand why you might do what you did, Lyla . . . Lyla—'

'Look,' interrupted Imelda, impatient that she should have lost Cat's attention. 'Look at this.' She unrolled the paper and held it up.

Everyone turned.

The room fell silent.

Cat quickly reached out to take Lyla by the shoulders and turn her away, but Lyla broke free and gestured with her hand.

'Give it to me, Imelda.'

She walked slowly and carefully towards Imelda, very slowly because her legs were shaking and might give way. Girls drew apart as she came, some holding out a hand to help steady her, for all could see that Lyla's heart was breaking.

'Give it to me,' whispered Lyla.

Imelda took a step back, and holding the paper up above her head in one hand, the letter in the other, she recited, '*The Hon. Florence Spence, artist and divorcee, flees the scandal in Britain caused by her affair with the German spy Heinrich Meier and begins a new life in America.*'

Lyla leaped forward and lunged for the paper and tore at it and found that she had in her hands only the front page. Frozen, she stared down at the picture of Mop, saw Mop's smile and curls, the large eyes, now rimmed with kohl, the white fur cape about her shoulders, new pearls about her neck that Lyla'd not seen before, and read again . . . *Begins a new life in America.*

Mop was in America. Without ever saying anything to Lyla.

Lyla made her way towards the stairs, clutched at the newel post and there, wracked by a sudden, violent spasm, she doubled over and vomited.

69

A DIFFERENT LIFE

In the morning Lyla heard hurried footsteps in the corridors, Ada calling for her, various doors being flung open, and finally Aunt Ada came to the door of Violet's room, where Lyla had gone to hide herself away.

Lyla, her face grubby with last night's tears, glanced covertly at her, then, begrudgingly and with apprehension, made space for her on the bed. Her aunt made herself comfortable, swinging her slippered feet up on to the bedspread.

They sat awhile in silence. Lyla toyed with shaking fingers at the hem of the sheet and, after some time, looked up at her aunt and whispered, 'I used to sit like this with Mop. Once upon a time, we'd sit together every morning, like this. She'd drink her tea and we'd make plans for the day.'

'Did you make her tea every morning?'

Lyla, remembering, nodded.

'Lyla . . .' Ada placed yesterday's letter from Mop

on her lap and drummed her fingers on it.

'Good God, child. How long has this been going on? How long have you been writing to yourself? I never knew – I had no idea . . .'

She folded Lyla in her arms and hugged and held her close, and in that hug Lyla felt something inside herself shift and soften. Ada whispered, 'Lyla, my poor child. She's not been at Lisson Square for months, Lyla, she left . . . Solomon went, you see, to find out where she had gone. Child, the letters you used to write to her, they probably never reached her . . .'

Ada took a deep breath.

'There's no right age to tell a child what I am forced by circumstances to tell you now . . . Lyla, the day your father brought you here, that was the day – the day your mother made her choice . . . when she chose . . . she chose a different life, she chose *not* to be a mother.'

Lyla began to tremble.

'What do you mean?'

'She asked your father to collect you, Lyla. She chose another life. Lovell never stole you from your bed; she'd asked him take you. On the eve of his departure for war, she asked him to take you from her.'

'To take me from her – what do you mean – she never said anything . . . she never *told* me.'

'I have no children, Lyla, and I'll never understand the decision she made, but it was just that – a deliberate decision . . . to leave you.'

'Why didn't you tell me? You – she – she never said – you never told—'

'How could I tell you, when you were so young, already so fierce and fragile? Even now, I barely have the strength—'

The habit of self-protection, so deep in Lyla, reasserted itself, and she turned on her aunt and burst out, 'It's because you wouldn't let me go back – if you'd let me – if you'd stopped a train . . .'

Aunt Ada was silent.

Mop will come back, Lyla told herself. *She was just escaping scandal, that was all. That was only natural. Anyone would want to do that.* But then Lyla glimpsed the cutting from Imelda's paper on the floor beside the bed and Mop's white cape and pearls. *Where had Mop got such a cape in a war, and who had given her the pearls. A new life? Did Mop want a new life? Did she want a life without Lyla? A life far away across an ocean?*

No. Lyla's shields and battlements rose and asserted themselves once more. *The newspapermen were wrong. They got everything wrong. Mop wouldn't leave a daughter alone in a country at war.*

Lyla began to hurl things across the room, anything she could lay her hands on, her book, her dressing gown and, to his astonishment and displeasure, Bucket's basket.

Ada, watching calmly, said, 'Tear it up. Tear the world to pieces, Lyla. It won't help in the long run, but it will be a temporary relief.'

70

AFTERWARDS

In all the free hours of the months that followed, Lyla – as much as she could – kept to herself, to her room, and, for company, to Bucket and Violet.

Dependable, she would say to herself sometimes. *Violet and Bucket are de-pen-da-ble.*

Cat came often to the door of the Yellow Silk Room, and each time Lyla would turn her away. She put a note under Lyla's door every morning, and others in snatched moments between lessons.

> *Lyla, please let me come in. I've always known about everything and don't mind about any of it, and I was only waiting for you to one day be ready to tell me the truth, and the only thing I do mind about is you not talking to me and I do miss you. Please talk to me.*
> *Cat xxx*

Like a sleepwalker, Lyla went through the motions of a timetable she knew by heart, sang the hymns, did

Prep and exams and played in matches. She studied, but only to lose herself in her work, receiving her grades in silence, burying herself in her books, going alone to the Orangery to draw, or sitting and reading by herself in Violet's room. Life passed over her as if she were a thing far beneath its surface. She heard all the familiar noises – the bells and the rushing footsteps, and all the clatter of a school going about its routine – as though she were underwater.

The girls kept their distance but smiled tentatively at her from time to time. Lyla turned her back on all of them. She lived on her own – half in the world of the girls, half out of it – missing things, arriving late, trailing things, dragging bags and dropping books, and generally lacking the information she needed to get her to the right place at the right time.

Sometimes she'd find a note on her desk.

Don't forget English Prep. By nine tomorrow.

Cat wrote again and again, and Lyla tore each missive up, throwing it into Bucket's basket till it was filled to the brim, and Bucket, resentful that his den had been mistaken for a wastepaper basket, *chuck-chucked* at her loudly.

Sometimes Lyla would say to herself as she threw in another scrumpled note, *I will keep myself on an even keel. My heart is all battlements and lookout towers and all*

71

THE ORANGERY

One evening Lyla found a note taped to her easel:

I SO MUCH WANT TO TALK TO YOU.
EVERYTHING IS SO MUCH LESS FUN
WITHOUT YOU.

Beside Lyla's charcoal lay a bar of chocolate.

That same evening Cat came to find Lyla in the Orangery. She bent to light the paraffin stove and said, 'You have to talk to me.'

'Why should I?'

Cat had grown taller and prettier and wiser still, and Lyla turned away, fear creeping by cold clutches up the battlements of her heart.

No one will love me. I am unlovable.

'I miss you, Lyla,' said Cat gently.

Lyla stared at Cat, who was calm and soft with sunlight, and felt she herself was all stone and shadow. 'No, you don't; no one does.'

'Your father hasn't written,' said Cat. 'For a long time, there's been no letter.'

'Why should I care?'

Cat bent to rake the embers of the stove, pausing for a moment, then turned suddenly with tears in her eyes and shook Lyla violently by the shoulders. 'You *should* care. You should!'

And with that, Cat released Lyla and stormed out, slamming the door and making all the Ancient Greeks tremble in their sandals.

72

IN THE KNOT GARDEN

One day in the spring, Great Aunt Ada led Lyla out into the knot garden where the girls were digging up the earlies. Lyla saw the girls turn to watch as Ada and she walked out into the park. They walked in silence a while till Aunt Ada turned a gaunt, stricken face to Lyla. 'You'll grow up very suddenly, I fear.'

'I am grown up,' retorted Lyla.

'Oh, not yet, you're not . . .' Ada stopped and turned and said directly, 'Lovell is missing, presumed dead. He was in a camp, Lyla, in North Africa, God help him, a German prisoner of war camp . . .' She watched Lyla's face. 'The camp was emptied when the Hun withdrew from Africa. Hitler moved his prisoners backwards with them as he retreated. Many of those at Hasufa were sent to Sforzacosta but Lovell's name has never reappeared on any list either in Germany nor Italy. We don't know what happened to him. His name is not on the list of prisoners at Sforzacosta.'

Lyla kicked at the grass.

'It's been a while, Lyla, since you received a letter. Did you never wonder about that?' Lyla stared at the ground and kicked at the grass again. Ada placed her hands on Lyla's shoulders. 'For a whole year, no letter from your father? From the man who wrote to you every single week?' She waited and watched.

Lyla felt the trembling in Ada's hands, their frailty, and wondered why it should be that all the strength of indomitable Great Aunt Ada should be running away so fast, like water through fingers.

'Did you not think about the boxes for prisoners? Who were they really for? They were for Lovell, Lyla . . . For all of them, but mostly for Lovell. Let us pray, Lyla, that just one of them, out of all the thousands that we sent, just one of them arrived.'

Lyla, still staring at the grass, felt her lip begin to tremble as she whispered, 'Where is he?'

'We don't know . . . That is . . . it's most unlikely . . . There is so much disease in those camps, so much hunger.'

Lyla shook herself and lifted her face to her aunt's. 'I don't care. I don't care about anything. I don't care. I don't care what's happened to him.'

73

SIXTEEN

Lyla heard the wake-up bell and rolled over, burying her face in her pillow. Then, slowly, very slowly and cautiously, she rolled back again. There'd been a papery rustling sound at her feet when she'd moved. She wiggled her feet and heard it again, felt the weight of something on the bedspread. Warily she sat up and paused, confused to see a large ribboned package and a card.

Her birthday. Today was her sixteenth birthday.

Bucket was all bushy-tailed and most intrigued by the parcel that had appeared on the bed in the night, but Lyla stretched out to pick up the card: a collaged drawing – created by many hands – of Violet and Bucket and Ada, with Dandelions embroidered in pink wool across the sky and signed inside by every Garden Hill girl that was at Furlongs. So much time and care had been lavished on the thing that tears started in Lyla's eyes. After a while she put the card aside and fingered the parcel. With Bucket's assistance, she undid the wrapping. Cat, for this was so thoughtful that it was surely Cat's work, had gathered together a new school uniform, art paper that wasn't brown, and a sock with a bell on it for Bucket.

Lyla lay back on her pillows, watching Bucket play with his sock and thinking how, having been so absent and withdrawn, she done so little to deserve such kindness.

She gazed out of the window, remembering that this was the fourth birthday she had spent at Furlongs. On each of those birthdays she'd waited by Trumpet and the mail tray. A card from Mother had never come. Not once. Today she would not wait for a letter. She had been given a beautiful card and a present and she would not so much as think of anything coming from Mother.

Lyla thought back over the years she'd spent at Furlongs, remembering how a birthday letter from Father had come, sooner or later one had always come, and always she'd waved it away. But today there'd be nothing from him. Perhaps there'd never be anything from him ever again. Lyla sat up and tensed. Those letters he'd sent, where were they? What had been done with them?

Slowly Lyla rose and walked to the window. She looked down to knot garden searching for the damson, remembering how she'd made Solomon turn Father's letters – letters written from harsh and lonely places –

into plans to send out into the garden.

Lyla started – if Father were alive and well, there'd be something from him today. Suddenly she turned from the window and ran. In her nightdress she raced down to the hall and grabbed at the in tray. Empty. The post had not yet come perhaps. She ran to the window and saw Mabel Rawle on the drive and ran out towards her, flinching and hopping over the gravel in her bare feet. Breathless and panting, she asked Mabel if there were one for her, and Mabel huffed and heaved and sorted through her bag . . . but no, there was nothing for Lyla Spence.

Lyla turned and walked slowly back to the house. She paused before the door, then suddenly, at a desperate thought, turned away to make her way instead to the walled garden. Lyla picked her way across the garden to the old damson and looked up into its branches, remembering how white those fighter planes, unwanted blossoms, had looked amidst its leaves.

She fingered the bark of the tree thoughtfully, and then suddenly took hold of a branch and swung herself up. She climbed higher up and then crawled along the branch, reaching and searching as she went for any tiny scrap that she might hold. There was nothing.

Nothing, not even a scrap that she might keep. Father had written week after week, year after year, to the daughter who'd turned so fiercely away from him, and now where was he? Had his life ended in a lonely German jail, ignored by the daughter he loved. Tears began to fall among the branches of the old damson.

As she wept, something landed on her shoulder. She started and batted at it to brush the bug away. But then another landed – she clutched at it. A paper letter plane. Another fell and then another and soon paper letter planes – in pinks and purples and all the colours of the rainbow were falling all about her. Caught in the branches of the damson and scattered in the grass all around were Spitfires and Hurricanes and Lancaster Bombers.

She looked up at the stone walls of Furlongs and saw the windows of all the dormitories were open and letter planes were flying out from them all, and that Violet had put her head out to eat her breakfast clematis with a coloured paper chain hung about her neck, and that an appliquéd banner was being strung from statue to statue of the pediment.

HAPPY BIRTHDAY, LYLA!

Lyla picked up a paper plane, unfolded it and read:

Lyla, we love you because you're fierce.

And another:

Lyla, we love you because you're funny.

More and more letter planes were falling, and the elderly damson transformed with glorious multicolour paper blossom. Lyla took one more:

*Lyla, we love you because you like
your letters to be sent into trees.*

She opened another and another. Every member of staff, every Garden Hill girl, even Solomon and Cedric, all of them had sent her a paper plane.

Lyla, we love you because you're brave.

Lyla stayed in the branches of the old damson clutching the planes as they fell and reading them but thinking of all the other letters, the letters from Father, that she'd never read.

74

PREPARING FOR VICTORY

Just as Ada's interest in parabolas and probability and Pink Dandelions had each, at some point, flagged, so the work with the Red Cross parcels had faded away. Ada had suddenly decided, too, that board games were no longer required by prisoners. *She is tired*, the girls said to one another. *It is too much for her.*

And yet, one day, some fitful, steely energy returned to Great Aunt Ada.

'We must prepare, prepare for Victory,' she announced. 'We must salvage something from this war. We must make flags. We must sew them in readiness for the day that will surely come. We will do sewing classes. I intend to instruct these classes myself, for it is high time I learned to sew and – you never know – I might find it comes in useful in the future.'

The girls watched Aunt Ada advance across the hall, holding in her arms a bolt of navy cloth. Solomon, always now two steps behind her, bore one bolt of red and another of white cloth. Ada's large, once confident stride had grown short and uncertain, her voice tremulous and reedy. Lyla saw then that Ada had grown old in gulps – not smoothly, but as if rushing towards the end. Her startling white hair stood upright in sparse tufts and she'd begun to resemble more closely now the effect of one of her own explosions. Cedric Tawny's handling of the shears as he set about her hair might have become a little inaccurate for he too had aged, but he'd say, by way of explanation, *She has no patience, she will not sit still.*

'I must see this through,' Aunt Ada muttered, plonking down the bolt of navy cloth. 'Must see the whole thing through.'

The girls grinned, for she spoke as if she were entirely responsible for marshalling Britain to Victory.

75

NEW YORK

'*Lyla Spence,*' announced Trumpet.

Lyla froze.

'Lyla Spence!' called Trumpet again.

Lyla rose to take her letter and the hall grew silent, for all knew that a letter for Lyla was a thing of note.

Mother's writing on the envelope.

The last time she'd seen Mother's handwriting had been so long ago.

Lyla turned the thing over and over again in her hands. The postmark was New York, the letter dated three weeks ago. Lyla stared at Mop's handwriting on the envelope, still familiar now. She heard the bell ring, heard girls rushing for the classrooms, and still she stared at the envelope.

Cat stood hesitantly at Lyla's side. 'Would you like me to stay with you?'

'It has come too late,' answered Lyla, and put the thing away, fearing it might detonate her and split her all to pieces.

Later, however, unable to cast it away, she read it alone in her room:

Dear Lyla,

I dock at Liverpool on the 2nd May. Please meet me off the SS America.

I shall make a better grandmother, one day, than I did a mother, and shall be able to give all the love and time that should have been for you to your children.

I will look for you on the dock.

Love,

Mop

76

A NEW COAT AND HAT

Lyla went to find her aunt and, hearing Cat's voice from the Smoking Room, she paused outside it, startled that Cat should be in there. She peered in and saw, side by side at the fire, Ada and Cat – Ada's hand in Cat's. Lyla hesitated, feeling an unaccountable resentment that they should both be sitting there, together, in a new alliance, which didn't seem to include herself.

'Your father might be able to help, perhaps, take that to him,' Great Aunt Ada said as she passed something to Cat.

Cat saw Lyla and she rose quickly, pocketing the paper. She went to the door and, as she passed Lyla, smiled, but Lyla raised her brows as if to ask, *And what were you discussing with my aunt?* But then Ada extended a hand in welcome to Lyla, and Lyla – remembering the letter from Mop and how she was coming home – said, 'I am going to Liverpool.'

Aunt Ada saw the letter in Lyla's hand and, after a

while, said with a warmth that had somehow also so much sorrow in it, 'Of course you are.'

'Will you ask the train to stop?'

'I shall call an entire train especially for you.'

'And will you come with me to Ladywood to help me choose a new coat and hat?' asked Lyla, smiling, because of course there was no knowing what sort of garments her Great Aunt Ada might select if one was to judge by the way she chose to dress herself.

'Of course, dear. Does Florence require you to be in a new coat and hat?'

Ada might be frail, but she could still be sharp.

'I'd like to look nice,' Lyla answered shyly.

Ada took a deep breath, then looked up and said breezily, 'Of course you would . . . Speck says you've an allowance, d'you know?'

'Speck?'

'Solicitor. Wills and bills and so forth. For myself and for Lovell. Yes, yes, Lovell made provision for you at some point or other. See Speck – he's been taking care of it all.'

'Father did?' asked Lyla.

Ada nodded. 'Of course.'

In Evanses, Ada was at her most majestic.

'Bring me all the best hats and all the best coats,' she told the assembled staff, sweeping her arms across the shop floor. 'The best of everything. She's going to

Liverpool, d'you know, and she must look her best. She's sixteen now,' Aunt Ada told the salesgirl. 'She came to me when she was just eleven or thereabouts. What were you, child . . . ?'

Lyla emerged from the changing room and walked slowly towards her aunt, displaying a fashionable, grown-up sort of coat.

Her aunt's eyes filled with tears. 'Show Solomon,' she said, flustered and too breezy. 'Call him in – call him in. He has a good eye.'

Solomon entered and said nothing and looked nowhere until Ada prompted him.

'Well, Solomon, what d'you think?'

Solomon gave one of his magical smile-drawing smiles and nodded gently, and everyone in Evanses was smiling.

'Very good, very good,' said Ada brusquely. 'We'll take it all, be quick about it, hat and coat and gloves and bag and so on.'

Back at Furlongs, Lyla showed Cat the new coat and hat.

'They're beautiful,' said Cat, fingering the ivory collar. 'Your mother should be so proud,' she whispered.

Lyla hugged her friend, but Cat withdrew a little, her eyes wide and deep with concern. 'I don't understand *why* you want to go – are you really sure about this?'

After a long pause, Lyla answered as best she could,

but only with a question. 'Cat, do you think the need to be loved by a parent ever leaves one – as you get older, I mean?'

'She doesn't deserve you, Lyla,' came Cat's reply.

It was Cat who accompanied Lyla to the little station, for Ada was unwell and supposed to be with the doctor. *Don't hold with doctors*, she'd said, waggling her fingers at him. *Off with you.*

'Dr Dean Seldom Seen,' Cat had whispered.

As they pulled up, Lyla saw the clock whose hands moved so slowly, and the solitary ewe that still grazed along the tracks, and she smiled. She then saw the worry in Cat's eyes.

'I'll be all right,' she told her friend, then waved and turned.

'Lyla – wait – Solomon has something – *we* have something for you,' Cat called after her.

Solomon limped towards Lyla and, bowing a little, he handed her a little rosewood box inlaid with ivory.

'Captain Lovell gave me this. In the last war.' He handed it over carefully. 'I was always proud to serve him.'

'We thought it was a good place, Lyla, to keep things in,' said Cat.

'Thank you,' replied Lyla, bemused.

The train was approaching, so Lyla waved once more and turned.

77

LIVERPOOL

There were several changes of trains, and Lyla, already confused by all the complexities of train and platform changes, was dazzled by the fact of a whole world having been going on all these years outside of Furlongs.

As she drew nearer to Liverpool, the newsprint image of Mop in pearls and white fur began to haunt Lyla. She took Mop's letter from her bag and read it once again. She read and re-read it and knew then that she was looking for something in it that was not there, for the things Mop had not asked: *How was Lyla doing? How had she fared all these long years? Who had clothed her and fed her? Who'd loved her failings and mistakes? Who'd laughed with her and cried with her and held her? Who'd told her all the unfathomable things you needed to know to be a grown-up?*

She remembered then what Solomon had said as she'd climbed into the pony trap. '*Captain Spence would be so proud, Miss Lyla . . . I was always proud to serve your father, miss.'*

Mop had not mentioned Father.

Lyla stuck her hands in her pockets and gazed out of the window. She thought of the Mail In and Mail Out trays and how she'd put so many letters in the out tray and how there'd never ever been one from Mop. The attendant came by and Lyla fumbled in her bag for her ticket.

She glanced down at the rosewood box and smiled and thought how quaint and sweet it was of Solomon to think to give her that just before she went on a journey.

'Are you meeting the *SS America* too?' a lady in Lyla's compartment asked.

Lyla nodded.

When she arrived at the station, Lyla hailed a cab and told the driver, 'To the docks, please.'

After a while he asked, 'The *SS America*?'

Lyla nodded.

'Father?'

Lyla shook her head, but the driver, sucking loudly on a boiled sweet, persisted.

'Brother home on leave?'

Lyla shook her head.

'Wounded and coming home then, from the East?'

Lyla hesitated, then replied, 'Father – he's – lost . . .'

The driver watched her in the windscreen mirror and waited.

'They don't know what happened to him,' whispered Lyla.

The driver said nothing for a while, then held out a Fox's glacier mint through the glass partition. Lyla took it and unwrapped it as he continued to watch her in the rear-view mirror. 'Who you meeting then? Someone special?' he asked.

Not once had Mother written.

Yet there was the rose-and-silver dress, the beautiful dress her Mother had chosen for her.

Slowly Lyla began to shake her head from side to side.

No. Not Mother.

The dress hadn't come from Mother. Mother had never sent a dress nor any single tiny thing.

Lyla shook her head again: no, that had been Ada's doing of course – Ada must have dispatched Solomon to Harrods. *He had a good eye. He knew about the staff in Harrods.*

With that admission, other things – scraps of memory, once somehow rubbed out – came floating back across the years, rising like faint ripples to the surface of water. *That last night in London? She's always on her own, Winnie had told the policeman. No, Father had never left Mop, it was never as Mop had told her it was. There had been no Ethel in Brighton . . .* Lyla writhed and covered her face as if in pain.

The driver, still watching her in his mirror, pulled over.

'All right, love?'

'Turn around,' Lyla commanded. 'Turn around and go straight back, please. Go very fast.'

Back at the station, she went straight to the ticket office.

'A single to London, please.'

78

LISSON SQUARE

Lyla's taxicab took her along the Marylebone Road. She saw lilac and ragwort amidst the rubble. She saw queues for fish and advertisements for Brylcreem. She saw exhaustion and defiance in the faces of the people on the streets, and she saw the newsstands saying that Victory would be soon be announced.

The cab turned into Lisson Square and Lyla saw the cart and the old mare that Southbridges, the bakers, kept behind the shop, still plodding round with her load of bread. 37 Lisson Square was just as it had always been in Lyla's mind, only in the front garden, around the cherry tree, were rows of carrots and potatoes where the lavender used to grow.

Lyla's hand paused on the bell. Through the bay window she saw dry stems in a silver vase, their fragile blooms long fallen. She saw a half-empty glass beside the gramophone and the scarf still on the centre table where Mop had left it that night, forgotten perhaps in the dizzy rush to leave.

The dizzy rush. The rush to another, different life; a life without a daughter.

Lyla lifted her finger from the bell and hesitated. She turned and went to the side passage and fumbled beneath the pot of winter jasmine for the spare key – and there it was, where it had always been, beneath the jasmine, which grew still as though there'd never been a war.

She turned the key, pushed the door and heard the rustle of papers. A pile of bills or pamphlets, perhaps, with instructions to travel at all times with a gas mask. She kicked the heap and trampled through it, dropped her bag, raced up the narrow stairs and flung open the door to Mop's room.

The mirrored wardrobes were open, the rails empty, the scent bottles on the dressing table gone. Lyle eyed the wardrobes, wondering. Had Mop already packed her clothes away when she'd left the house that last night?

Lyla paused. If she had ever known that those wardrobes had been empty – if she had glimpsed them so that night – then that must have been a knowledge too unbearable for the child she had been. That was a knowledge that she had scrubbed out and banished from her mind.

Lyla turned abruptly, shut the door behind her and leaned against it, her chest heaving. From where she stood she could see directly into the room that had been her own, could now see the embroidered sampler on the wall, the pillow still with the imprint of a young child's head, the indent on the mattress where she'd lain that night curled tightly up.

Lyla backed away.

Up another flight of stairs, she found Mop's attic studio desolate, the easel, the oils, palette and brushes all gone. Mop had chosen that one part of her life, no, two parts, her painting and her clothes. She'd chosen to take those and to leave her daughter behind.

Lyla went to the drawing room and looked about. Where had she sat that night while she'd waited for Mop to return? Lyla walked slowly to the armchair by the telephone table in the window and, quivering, placed herself gingerly on it. She turned to look out on to the square. Here. Here was where she'd sat that night, tear-stained and trembling, watching for the motorcar that might bring her mother home.

Lyla closed her eyes. After a while she shivered and drew her legs up and wrapped her arms about them and rocked herself to and fro. This was where she'd sat all that long night. Why? Lyla, her eyes still shut, cast herself back. She'd taken herself to bed when Mop had left, and then she'd woken some time during the night and gone to Mop's bedroom and found no one there. She'd felt her way along the corridor and down the stairs, her fingers skimming the dado rail as she'd called out to her mother. She'd gone to the drawing room and there'd been no Mop.

She'd waited and waited in this very chair, waited and watched through the window, and in the end, terrified, she'd picked up the telephone and dialled the only number a very young child might know by heart.

The police had come and someone had put her on his knee. Someone big with hairy ears, and he'd asked, *Where was her father? Where was her mother?*

Remembering, Lyla winced and rocked herself to and fro.

She'd pulled away from Hairy Ears and thrown herself to the carpet, and there, crumpled on the floor, she'd sobbed. 'She goes out . . . She leaves me here . . . and if I wake, sometimes she's here, sometimes she's not . . .'

They'd looked from one to another.

A neighbour had been woken and then it was the neighbour perhaps who'd sent for Winnie, for Winnie had come, an overcoat over her pink dressing gown, blue rollers in her hair.

'*The child's* always *on her own. Night after night,*' Winnie had told the police.

She'd helped them trace Father to some underground part of Whitehall where things of the most secret nature were discussed through all the hours of the night, and then Winnie had returned Lyla to her bed and, as dawn broke, Father had been there at her bedside. He'd lifted her kicking and screaming from the bed and stepped out into the corridor. Mop's door had been open and Lyla had clutched at it, calling to her, but Father had walked swiftly on. Lyla remembered how he'd tucked a blanket round her in the seat of the Austin, his face drawn and haggard in the grey light of a London morning.

Lyla opened her eyes and saw the garden of Lisson Square. She shivered again and unfurled herself from the chair and looked about, and everything was as it always had been – the trinkets and the gilded frames and whatnots – only now everything was corroded and tinny to her eyes, and it was only the cobwebs that caught the evening sun.

She must leave, she must get out of this house, but an envelope on the floor by the door drew her eye. She saw the childish, careful block capitals. Trembling, she bent and took it up and slowly opened it:

Everyone has written home for their skates, so please, please will you send mine. I'm all right at ice skating and it's easier to make friends if you can be good at something . . .

Suddenly she was frantic, on her knees in the empty house, scrabbling through the mail, clutching up twenty – perhaps thirty – letters to her lap, tearing at them and reading, in painful, heart-wrenching snatches the words of the child she'd been, feeling once again through them the thousand hurts and slights, the hopes and fears and knowing, through the words she'd written, a longing for love so intense that even now it could rush up in her and take her by the throat.

PLEASE, PLEASE, DON'T FORGET ABOUT ME. DON'T LEAVE ME HERE FOREVER.

Somewhere upstairs a pigeon must have been trapped, for there was a flapping and the sound of glass breaking. When the light faded Lyla simply lay down, amidst the dusty envelopes, and drew her coat over her, for the electricity had long since been cut off and she had nowhere else to go.

79

BRITISH FIGHTER PLANES

In the morning Lyla struggled to her feet. She must find something to eat, she must find a change of clothes. She should return to Furlongs, for Ada was growing weak and old, her strength sapped surely by fear for Father. Lyla walked stiffly, for her sleep had been fitful and uncomfortable, to the drawing room and rifled through her bag to find what money was left. She must call Speck and make arrangements to collect some cash at a London bank.

As she looked for her purse, her finger snagged on the catch of the rosewood box. She winced and withdrew her hand, then paused, for the box had sprung open. She glimpsed white paper. She snatched the box from the bag and lifted it and out tumbled, on to the table amidst the withered tulips and half-empty glasses of that dreadful night, a host of tiny paper planes, Spitfires and Hurricanes, Vickers Wellingtons and Lancaster Bombers. Every letter Father had ever sent, from every desert and far-off place, turned by

Solomon's sorcery into paper planes. Someone had saved them all, fetched them from the damson tree and kept them for Lyla for when she was ready to read them.

Lyla's fingers hovered over the small paper planes, so light and delicate they were songbirds come from far away, only to be cast aside by a child more fragile still than they.

Lyla gathered them up and clasped them in her arms and sank into the chair at the window. She took first one and read, took another and another, and read and read on with pain and joy, with tears and smiles, till each letter was unfolded, the words of each unfurled, all the tenderness of them settling inside her like warmth and light. She read and read again, taking up first one and then another, reading and re-reading till she was washed through with tears.

One last letter lay at the bottom, flat and unfolded.

Campo Concentramiento 53
Sforzacosta
Italy

Dear Lyla,

If we meet again, we'll meet as strangers, for you'll be so much changed. One day, when all this is over, and you are old enough, there is much I have to tell you. I miss so many things, but what I most miss is you. Dear Lyla, remain whole-hearted. Don't let anything or anyone take from you the parts of you that are most you.

We, all of us, are feeling stronger now the spring is coming. The sun is a great help for we have been so cold, so hungry – but we get parcels now and again from the Red Cross and it is marvellous what one can find in them. There is a gate made of wood, the height of two men, flanked by windowless buildings and steel spikes and then two fences draped with barbed wire. I can see it from the small, high window of our cell. The guards are slack and dozy, drinking at their posts. I observe their comings and goings from the little window. They have lost heart for this war, the Italians, if their heart was ever in it at all.

This may be my last letter for a while. If I make it out of here, my journey could be long and dangerous. I will have little to help me on my way bar some Ambrosia rice and other most amusing but helpful things sent by the Red Cross.

I plan to take the long way home, so to speak. Pray for me.

If I make it back, perhaps one day you'll see I did the only thing I could. Either way, whatever you think of me,

I will always, always be your Father

80

LORD NORTH STREET

Lyla replaced the key beneath the winter jasmine.

She telephoned Speck and asked for money to be arranged and was told that Ada had had a minor stroke. *Come back as soon as you can,* Speck told her.

Where did my Father live? What was his regiment? *Ah, as it happens, I do have that information.*

Father. Father, who'd once pretended to have an affair for the sake of Mop's reputation, what home had he made for himself then? For Lyla didn't recall being taken there. *Try the Records Office too,* Speck told her. *Start there.*

Lyla replaced the receiver in its cradle.

At the Records Office there were long queues, long waits. Father was not among the lists of wounded, nor of the dead. *Try his barracks,* she was told, and at the barracks they said to Lyla, *Ah yes, others have been asking after Lovell Spence too. We are following leads and searching; we have not given up hope.* Lyla discovered that the camp at Hasufa had indeed been closed after El Alamein, the Germans, had indeed moved their prisoners on, some to Germany and some to Northern Italy. *Yes, Lyla*, told the officer, *he was in Italy, at Sforzacosta. How did she know?* the officer asked, and Lyla showed him Father's letter. *That is helpful*, she was told. *We shall keep searching but you should also try Baker Street, go to the office in Baker Street – he worked for them too, and they might well know more.*

Lyla saw the sheep in Hyde Park, the people eating off check oilskin tablecloths in cafes, advertisements for Elastoplast, the hansom cabs still on Park Lane.

Next day, at the Baker Street offices, Lyla found a secretary packing away files into cardboard boxes, disbanding the small office, but she knew no more than Lyla did.

The camp at Hasufa was closed, Lyla was told once again. *After that the trail goes cold. Some perhaps were sent to Germany and some to Italy but Lovell Spence was a special case. The enemy would have hung on to him, you know; they knew how valuable he was to us, a clever man, Lovell Spence.* Lyla told her he'd been at Sforzacosta.

We did know that. The secretary pursed her lips and paused. *In fact, there was a breakout, shots were fired. We are concerned. We'd like him back; we have people searching for him. The others – those who got away – headed, we think, for the Adriatic, but that would have been dangerous for it was still in German hands.*

Lyla thanked the secretary and made her way to

the address Speck had given her in Lord North Street. The doorman showed her in. Father had never spent much time in this apartment. How lonely he must've been in this cheerless place, forced out of sweet Lisson Square by a divorce he'd never wanted, his name in the courts and in the press.

There was a desk, a single chair and bookshelves. Lyla ran her fingers along their dusty spines. No histories or manuals. Novels, more novels, plays and poetry. Dickens and Shakespeare. Lyla smiled.

She pushed the door to the bedroom and saw a desk, and on it a photograph of herself taken in the garden at Lisson Square. She was on Father's shoulders and Mother was beside them.

When she went back down, the doorman was waiting for her. He'd remembered, he told her, that someone else had come asking for him – he couldn't remember who – a solicitor perhaps. Did Lyla know that there was to be an exhibition, that woman, a show of her paintings? He handed Lyla the *Evening Standard. You could ask her*, he suggested. *She might know; she was his wife once.*

Lyla took it and read. Swiftly she folded it and handed it back. She lifted her head. Mother had come to Britain, not to see Lyla, but to celebrate the opening of a new exhibition in Albemarle Street.

Lyla thanked the doorman, left the apartment and made her way through gathering crowds to Albemarle

Street. There she peered through the narrow bow-front window. Mop might be there.

Lyla drew back and waited a while. She saw that the gallery owner was watching her to see if she'd come in or if he should shut up shop. Lyla slunk quietly in and walked in a trance through the two small rooms and saw the dark, angry works, all greens and blacks, and occasional whites, jagged and unsettling as loose teeth or broken bones.

At the back of the gallery, however, a small figure drawing in crayon drew her eye, and as Lyla approached, she saw beneath it the words *Not for Sale*.

Lyla caught her breath. She saw herself in that drawing, herself as a young child, perhaps five or six, standing on tiptoe, holding a palette towards the onlooker, her eyes earnest and upwards-looking. Lyla paused, seeing all the trust and the love in the child's eyes, then she turned on her heel and marched out.

Lyla woke on the morning of May the 8th to the news that war would end in Europe. The newsstands reported that at Eisenhower's headquarters at 2.41 a.m., Germany had unconditionally surrendered all land, air and sea forces in Europe to the Allies.

There could be a brief period of rejoicing.

Everywhere people were huddled around wireless sets, the shops were filling with buttonholes and flags, and ladders emerged from buildings, appearing from nowhere as if they'd been always there these five long years, waiting in readiness for the time that would surely come for flags and pennants and bunting to be hung from the rooftops.

In Trafalgar Square, people splashed in the fountains, some children rode the lions, while others atop their fathers' shoulders waved flags. Lyla saw a young girl, her hair tied in a red-white-and-blue ribbon on the top of her head. She watched the girl and thought of the photograph she'd seen, and how she too had once sat on a father's shoulders.

Huge crowds had gathered everywhere and you couldn't put a pin between the people on the streets. Lyla was caught up in the surge towards the palace and heard the clamouring at the gates for all the comings and goings of the king and the princess and the prime minister. Lines of loudspeakers were being rigged along the roads for the announcements and for the street parties that would come later.

She heard Churchill's voice: '*Advance, Britannia! Long live the cause of freedom. God save the King.*'

The bells pealed out all over London from every tower and spire. The traffic was at a standstill; there was kissing and singing and smiles and tears. Someone somewhere was playing an accordion, and Lyla was swept up into a conga line, then twirled and kissed.

Suddenly, violently, Lyla wanted to be at Furlongs with those with whom she'd spent the war, with Cat and with Ada. She broke away from the crowds into Green Park and began to run, across Hyde Park, through Lancaster Gate running and running, till she reached Paddington Station.

81

RIBBONS AND FLAGS

Lyla finally reached Furlongs in the late afternoon of the following day.

Everything was much as it had been when she'd first come: the elms and the bracken, the boathouse at Shearwater, the primroses and the sheep.

But then she saw a sheep that was red and she rubbed her eyes and looked away. She paused, then looked back again, and saw that, indeed, several were red, that, indeed, others were blue, that others were still white and she smiled.

The house came into view. From every window and from every tower and turret hung Ada's homemade Union Jacks, and there were ribbons and draperies, and every marble goddess on the pediment wore a blue bra and red knickers, and Violet at the maharajah's window wore bunting about her neck. On the lintel of the door perched a row of doves, most huffy that they had somehow turned red. Lyla saw others that had been coloured blue, and it appeared they were painfully embarrassed by the colour they now found themselves to be, for they had taken themselves off in shame to the weather vane. Only the doves that were still white remained on the clock tower where they should be.

Lyla grinned. *Dear Aunt Ada. Where was she? How was she?*

She found Tawny first at the foot of an immense bonfire. He greeted her, with his habitual reticence, raising a hand to his victory rosette.

'They died for *something*, my boys.'

'They did,' said Lyla, hugging him. Then she pulled back and whispered, 'Ada?'

He bowed his head. 'Another stroke.' He shook his head sadly.

Another stroke? Lyla had only been away three days.

She went to find Solomon.

'Miss Lyla . . .' he began, but his words seemed to turn to wood in his mouth and he, who'd always been so correct, who'd held himself in such reserve, bent his head to hide his tears.

Lyla remembered his moustache, how he'd used to try to make her smile, how all those years he'd always been at Ada's side, and she remembered Father's letters too, and she took his hands in hers.

'The letters, Solomon. Thank you.'

'It was Miss Lively who climbed the tree to fetch them down again,' he replied, gesturing apologetically to his legs. 'She always said we must keep them and wait till you were ready to read them.'

Lyla smiled. *Dear Cat.* 'Thank you, Solomon.'

'It was for him I did it too. There is nothing I would not do for Captain Lovell, miss. Did you hear anything of him in London?'

Lyla shook her head.

They left the conversation there, and together went in search of Ada.

They found her at last, being pushed about the park by Cat. She was sitting in a homemade sort of contraption – a tapestry wingback chair – to the base of which Tawny, perhaps, had fixed the wheels of his barrow and to the back a handle. On Ada's lap was a pair of secateurs.

Cat greeted Lyla with a hug, before she and Solomon left Lyla to be alone with her aunt.

Ada waggled the fingers of her right hand at all the adjustments to the facade of the house and to the bonfire that stood in front of it and, with great effort, whispered, 'A final fling, d'you see?'

Lyla paled.

'The girls . . . they're orf. New school ready, prefabricated . . .' Ada's words were halting and slow. 'Went up in a jiffy, like a mushroom – they do that these days, put things up overnight, not like this old place . . . progress, yes . . . take me to the roses . . . legs, d'you see, won't hold me up, want to see my roses –'

They went about the roses and after a while Ada said, 'I liked having 'em here, you know, the girls. Bonfire tonight for 'em . . . For them – and for England.'

'I couldn't find anything,' said Lyla eventually. 'They don't know if he got out, if he was hit . . .' Then with a rush of anger she asked Ada, 'Why didn't you say? Why didn't you make me see? There were so many things I didn't see.'

'How could you see? One sees things only . . . only when one is ready,' croaked Ada. 'Besides, you are young and much can happen . . . There is time. There are things in hand – people searching – Whitehall, Baker Street, Speck, Mr Lively – yes, yes, people searching . . .' She hesitated, visibly exhausted. But then her face brightened and she added, 'The long reach of your old great aunt,' she added.

Lyla smiled, for the fine, indomitable spirit, the fight and the hope, was even now in Ada. She smiled too to think that Cat's father too should be searching for Father.

That night all the people from Ladywood came to Ada's victory fire, as did all the staff of Garden Hill for Girls, and all the girls, and Cedric and Solomon. Prudence handed out hot soup and they sang the National Anthem. Ada was wheeled forward to light the branches of the bonfire. A great sheet of flame shot up into the darkening sky and everyone clapped and Violet whinnied from an upstairs window, for she had never seen such things. They laughed and linked hands – staff and girls, Solomon, Cedric and Prudence – and sang 'Auld Lang Syne'. Lyla and Cat stood together watching the flames of the bonfire light up the park and sky.

'I'll remember it all,' said Cat. 'You know, forever, every tiny bit of it. The snowdrifts in a bathroom, a ballroom laid to turf for a horse, chilblains, chestnuts, blackberries and frozen ink . . .'

Lyla took Cat's hand. 'I am told we'll remember only the joy and the pain,' she said solemnly. 'I have been much improved, you know. I have received a rooftop lecture from a great aunt, and I have read letter planes from far-off places . . . I read . . .' Lyla glanced towards the damson, which was lit in a flickering, fitful red, and in the darkness tears trickled down her cheeks. Turning her face towards Cat and looking her in the eyes, she whispered brokenly, 'Oh, Cat, I read those letters . . .'

Cat encircled Lyla in her arms.

Lyla, her head on Cat's shoulder, whispered through her tears, 'I do everything wrong, make all the wrong choices—'

'I hope *I'm* not one of your wrong choices,' said Cat, laughing to make light of things. 'Anyway, sometimes life gives you the chance to undo your mistakes, you know, and you must promise me that if it does, that if life does give you that chance, you will take it.'

82

SWINGING ON A STAR

The girls were led inside, Lyla wheeling Ada in her chair at the head of them all, and Lyla saw that stacks of trunks stood packed and ready around the edges of the Painted Hall. The girls would go, and she – what would she do? Where would she go? She would not stay at Furlongs if there were no Ada here to make sheep red and doves blue and dandelions pink.

Girls were taking places on their trunks, the youngest on the bottom row, the older girls like Cat and Lyla scrambling to the top, and all the Painted Hall was filled, and Prudence went about with bowls of sausages.

From her wheelbarrow chair, Ada summoned Cat with a waggle of her fingers. They whispered and nodded, and Lyla saw that since she'd gone they'd formed some new understanding to which she was not privy. A little put out, she asked Cat as Cat clambered back up, 'What were you saying to her?'

Cat answered evasively, 'Oh, I don't know – timings

for our departure tomorrow, that sort of thing. I am leaving early, you know.'

Great Aunt Ada waggled the fingers of her right hand at the console table. Solomon wheeled her over and Great Aunt Ada again waggled her fingers. 'Unveil it, Solomon.'

Solomon, as though he were opening a new church or a museum, pulled aside a dust sheet, and the girls gathered, thrilled to see a gramophone at Furlongs.

Ada, beaming from ear to ear, croaked, 'Frightfully up to date, d'you see.'

The girls smiled at one another, for gramophones had been popular in places other than Furlongs for at least twenty years.

Solomon put the needle down and from the trumpet speaker came Glenn Miller, and the feet of even the most whiskery-bosom-to-belly staff began to tap, and the girls were delighted.

Primrose took Cedric's hand and together they danced the Lindy Hop. And Lyla, sitting with Cat, giggled, for everyone – even The Rector Scott Talks Rot – was tapping their feet, and then Prudence was dancing with Dr Dean Seldom Seen, and there was joy and fight in Ada still, for when she saw Prudence dance she called for Solomon to wheel her out and push and pull her to the beat, and she herself waggled her right arm and right foot to the rhythm of some entirely different dance of some other era while Little

Gibson, who knew nothing of wars and victories, shook himself and looked about, resentful at such commotion.

Bing Crosby sang 'Swinging on a Star', and Primrose kicked off her shoes, and then there was Doris Day and 'Lili Marlene', and all the girls and all the staff – even Threadgold – danced, and Lyla saw, for the first time, how much the staff had given up to be there at Furlongs all through the war, and how much personal sacrifice was perhaps involved.

There was rum and Coca-Cola and Tommy Dorsey and Anne Shelton and Vera Lynn and, at the end of it all, when Prudence brought in hot chocolate and the gramophone played 'The White Cliffs of Dover', Great Aunt Ada waggled her fingers at the Great Stairs and to the ramp constructed out of old blackboards, that now ran from the foot of the Painted Hall to the landing at the top.

'Bedtime. A ramp, d'you see? Practical and most convenient. You might ask Violet if she'd like to come down that ramp – not till I am gone, mind you, it's comforting to have a horse at hand . . .'

Lyla scrubbed the tear from her cheek.

Her great aunt took her hand. 'One of the many improvements you have bought to the place, Lyla.'

Lyla smiled, and she and Solomon together, somehow, got Ada and the wheelbarrow chair up the blackboard ramp.

83

FOR SHE'S A JOLLY GOOD FELLOW

Next morning, Dr Dean Seldom Seen came to tell Lyla that Great Aunt Ada had taken a turn for the worse, another stroke. Lyla saw how the girls were scattered all about the house, going through the rooms with Brownie cameras, chattering excitedly to one another, their minds already on their homes and families. Lyla saw through a window how the desks were gathering around the fountain on the forecourt, tables, chairs, lockers, hockey sticks. The girls in burgundy were leaving just as suddenly as they'd once come.

Where was Cat? Lyla searched the house, asking everyone she passed, but no one knew – they were distracted, their minds already on their homes and families and on the prefabricated school building in Garden Hill. Lyla asked again and again and it was only Brenda who knew anything.

'Oh, I heard your aunt called for her.'

Lyla would go to Ada, but first she would fetch Violet to bring to her.

'Great Aunt Ada wants you close at hand,' she whispered to the horse, as she led her into the corridor.

At Ada's door, Violet paused and whinnied. Ada turned and her eyes were bright with tears as Lyla led gentle Violet up to the bed.

'Ah, dear Violet.'

Violet nosed Ada, and Ada happened to find she had a carrot about her person, so Violet stayed at her side and never once went to the window in search of climbing plants.

Lyla sat beside Ada on her remarkably narrow and uncomfortable bed and asked why she herself had had so grand a room.

'No point having unicorns if you're too old to ride them. No, no – they had to be for you.'

'You've never been old,' said Lyla.

'No good for anything now – less than half of me'll do what I want it to.'

'Aunt Ada, have you seen Cat?'

'Gone,' replied her aunt. 'Business to attend to. She's a good friend to you.'

The sound of singing rose up from outside, and Lyla went over to the window and saw that the entire school and staff had gathered beneath Ada's window. She pulled up the casement so Great Aunt Ada could hear that she was a 'jolly good fellow'.

The girls boarded the buses and took their seats

and gazed at the house and began to wave through the windows and then to sing:

> When school days are long gone and friends far
>   apart
> We will carry the debt to these days in our heart
> We will remember the hopes and fears
> The joys and the laughter we shared all these years.
> The rights and the wrongs, the slights and the tears
> The triumphs and songs, the dreams and the fears
> We will ask, *Were we gentle and brave? Were we bold?*
>   *Were we strong?*
> *Did we have courage and kindness and truth*
> *When we stood hand in hand with the friends of*
>   *our youth?*

Lyla waved and Violet whinnied and Ada murmured, 'Not their strong point, singing.' With a lopsided but twinkling, triumphant smile, she added, 'Never mind, brought Pinners into line, didn't we? Won a war, and so on.'

OLD ENGLISH ROSES

Lyla and Violet stayed by Ada's bedside through all that day.

Whenever the clock struck one or seven, Solomon appeared with a silver tray. Ada could neither sit up nor eat, but the courtesy that flowed like ancestral blood in her veins prompted her to whisper from time to time, so that he might feel he was of use, 'Don't leave . . . not till I'm gone . . . might be in need of a thing or two at any moment, eh, Solomon?'

She clasped her hands over the sheets, much in the manner she used to when waiting for dinner in the Smoking Room. Her pulse grew slow and faint . . . but just when it seemed to be fading completely, she'd come violently back to life, and croak and waggle her fingers at Solomon.

'Shipshape . . . get me shipshape – Tawny for my hair.'

Lyla and Solomon conferred and decided that, on balance, Tawny and his shears were not appropriate to the circumstances, so Lyla went to the dressing table and found a brush, which looked suspiciously like it might once have belonged to Violet.

Lyla had set about brushing her aunt's hair when Ada croaked, 'Pointing this way – must face the old house . . . must have Solomon to hand, keep an eye on you all . . .'

Through her tears, Lyla glimpsed on Ada's small, tidy table a photograph of a young man, bespectacled and awkward, beside him a striking girl with a high forehead and laughing eyes. Lyla held it up and mouthed at Solomon, 'Who?'

'Dr Reginald Gibson,' Solomon whispered.

Gibson? Lyla glanced at Little Gibson the canary on the bedhead.

Solomon smiled and nodded. 'A keepsake. She told me Reginald once gave her a canary and ever since—'

'I see,' said Lyla, because, for once, she did suddenly see that her great aunt had once been a young girl herself. Gradually Lyla adjusted herself to such a notion. 'Did she love him very much?'

Solomon nodded. 'I believe so, Miss Lyla.'

'Why didn't they marry?'

He shook his head and gestured about to indicate the house and grounds and then to a portrait over the mantel, and by all this gesturing Lyla understood that Ada's family had thought Reginald Gibson was too 'below-stairs' a person for the daughter of an earl, and, Lyla supposed, she'd never married since because she'd only loved Reginald, and perhaps that was why she'd lived so long alone, dining on Welsh rarebit at seven only in the company of her horse.

The hours passed, and – having the vague notion that such a thing was usually done at such a time – Lyla mouthed to Solomon, 'Should we call Father Scott?'

'No, I think not, Miss Lyla – she never held much with priests.'

'All right. No priest.'

Prudence wept and buried her face in her patterned apron, and Tawny came with an armful of Ada's Old English Roses, all yellows and pinks and apricots, varied and rich and glorious. He laid them at her feet and no one could speak for grief.

Lyla stayed throughout that night by Ada's side. Solomon came at eight with toast for Little Gibson, an apple for Violet and a devilled kidney for his mistress. Gently Solomon woke Lyla. She rubbed her eyes and blinked and blinked again, for the sun had bloomed so brightly on the white sheets around Ada that they cast her blossomy light back at Lyla. The sheets were still.

Ada had gone, the manner of her going more peaceable than anything she'd set her mind to in life.

85

SPECK

Little Gibson refused toast and cuttlebones and all manner of delicacies and was inconsolable. He took himself off to the roses at Ada's feet, hid his head under his wing and would not hear of moving. Together Lyla and Solomon led poor sad-eyed Violet out of Ada's room and, with great quantities of apple, coaxed her down the blackboard ramp. Then Lyla, to the best of her ability, set about the funeral arrangements.

Among the various dubious pieces of advice she'd been given over the years by those that surrounded her, she remembered a favourite of Mop's: *Half of everything is in the preparation.* So she began with a list of those who might attend. After much thought, she came up with:

Solomon
Tawny
Prudence
Dr Gibson (if it is possible to find him)

The Rector Scott Talks Rot
Dr Dean Seldom Seen
Speck
The people from Ladywood
Cat (hopefully)

Dr Gibson would be hard to identify, but Lyla would try her best. She went to Prudence and found her in a high state of indignation in the kitchen. Prudence's tin hat was now relegated to the shelf above the fireplace, and to and fro amidst the copper pans and the tin hat went poor flustered Henny, who had of course stopped laying just when Prudence was in need of an egg or two for a funeral tea.

'In mourning, that hen. Cleverer than you or I, she be,' declared Prudence.

'Prudence, who was Reginald Gibson?'

Prudence put down her rolling pin and eyed Lyla. She plumped herself down on a chair, settled her immense bosom on the surface of the pastry table, took off her shoes to rub her bunions and began:

'Terrible awful time, that were. The old earl, he were a one, her father, he fetched his daughter back – knew all along university for a girl were a mistake – Ada runned away – the old earl, he fetched her back and so on and in the end she stayed, but if she couldn't 'ave that scientist fellow Dr Gibson, she weren't going to take no other neither.' Prudence giggled. 'Frightened off every man in the county.'

'You never told me any of this before,' said Lyla.

'You never asked.' Prudence put her hands on her hips. 'Aye, we was all skippy and frolicsome in our day – it's only the young as never stop to think about what we was up to once.'

Lyla didn't want to hear just then about Prudence's skippy, frolicsome times, and thought she might go instead and see Father Scott Talks Rot.

'Ah well,' concluded Prudence as Lyla turned to leave, 'she lived in her own way in the end though . . . Invented summat that Dr Gibson did, some special bomb what skips or jumps or summat.'

Father Scott Talks Rot had suggested Lyla place a notice in *The Times* and go to see Mr Speck in the office above the chemist's in Ladywood. Lyla found that Speck's office had a log fire and a brass drinks trolley and piles and piles of books that were not about the law at all. He told Lyla that Ada's next of kin was, in fact, Lovell Spence, and after much searching eventually located a folder in which there was nothing but a small note that appeared to have been written on the back of a bill from the hardware store. '*After Lovell*,' Speck read aloud from the note, '*Furlongs could go to Miss Lyla Spence, should she care for it. I never had a child of my own till I had her.*'

'Father is missing, presumed dead.'

Speck told her that he himself had been making

investigations, that Lovell Spence was known to have escaped from Sforzacosta, that two other prisoners had escaped at the same time, but they had got separated from Lovell in the Adriatic somewhere. Speck was about to say more, but then he seemed to think better of it. After a second or two he looked up and smiled and said, 'Oh well, your great aunt has had everyone following up every lead everywhere – the Adriatic, Gibraltar, Spain, North Africa.' He smiled again. 'She was always most *thorough*.'

Lyla, who had spied a telephone inside one of Speck's desk drawers, asked if she might make a call and if he might help her look up a number.

When her call was answered, Lyla announced hesitantly, 'Hello, I'm calling for Cat. This is Lyla Spence.'

'Oh, I know who you are,' said a bright voice.

'Robin?' asked Lyla.

'Yes, but I'm not to talk to you,' he said very promptly.

'Not talk to me?' echoed Lyla, then she told him, 'Cat left without saying goodbye.'

'I'm not to talk to you,' repeated Robin stoutly. 'There's a reason,' he added, 'but it's secret, and I'm not to talk to you, so I can't tell you what it is, but I would if I could.'

'Oh,' said Lyla. Then, turning away from Mr Speck, she whispered into the receiver, 'Tell Cat . . . tell her, thank you. For *everything*. Tell her even if she never says hello or goodbye or anything else to me ever again . . . tell her I will always, *always* be her friend.'

'I can't do that because I'm not to talk to you.'

Robin was very earnest and very literal-minded, and Lyla wasn't getting anywhere with him, so she ended the call and turned to Speck.

'There is another thing – Aunt Ada had a friend. A Dr Reginald Gibson. He would want to know that she's gone.'

Mr Speck raised his brows. 'Ah yes. Interesting. A good, clever man. My second cousin more or less, as it happens – and actually he might help us. Ah well, very sad all that. He and Ada, you know . . . he never married again either.'

86

THE BILLIARD ROOM

From her wardrobe, Lyla selected a sober jersey and skirt. Soon she must go and walk behind her Great Aunt Ada to the chapel at Heaven's Gate, but first she would wander through Furlongs one last time.

She stood in the empty hall, listening to the silence of the house. Growing conscious that someone or something was watching her, she turned to the hall table and to Old Alfred, because it was, of course, Old Alfred who was watching her. There he'd stood, all these years, on his tiptoes, still between the Mail In and the Mail Out trays, watching and knowing.

Lyla drifted through the empty rooms, wondering if Ada's spirit might decide to stalk the corridors, gelignite in hand. She smiled, for if Ada returned to haunt her house, she'd be laughing as she went about, for Ada had lived with gusto, with ferocity, with joy and ready laughter.

Lyla wandered along the first-floor corridors and paused by Sir Galahad and placed her hand on his forearm and nodded to him. 'Farewell, friend.'

In the Red Library she saw on the dust of the windowpane the words she'd once thumbed:

PLEASE, PLEASE, COME FOR ME.

As she traced the letters once more with her finger, all the longing of those years, the longing to be loved, came rushing back to her, the yearning, the waiting, the hoping.

She raised her eyes and looked out and saw the boathouse at Shearwater and the lake, and remembered lying there with Cat on lyrical foxglovy afternoons, the blackberrying, the blustery acorn and chestnut times, the leaping joys, the larking on the rooftops, the Ancient Greeks in scarves, and the disgrace of the mathematics exam.

Lyla paused. She remembered the hall filled with girls, heard the echoing of the hymns they'd sung, the anthems and the carols, she heard the shrieks and laughter from the lake and in all these things she felt the sad slipping of the years that had gone.

Five wild, magical, lonely, tragic years.

At the door to the Billiard Room she paused, then pushed it open. Solomon had been busy clearing things, for the gelignite and blasting powder, strontium carbonate, string and tape and all the things devised to confuse German shipping were now gone.

Lyla ran her fingers along the baize surface of the billiard table at which she'd spent many long, dark evenings with Cat, filling boxes for the Red Cross. She turned and saw the Monopoly sets, stacked one above another, and smiled fondly at this eccentric notion of her great aunt's that British prisoners should want to play Monopoly so much more than any other game when they were bored and far away in foreign jails.

Why Monopoly?

Still wondering, Lyla walked slowly to the forbidden part of the room. She lifted a box from a package and placed it on the table. Why this game? Why couldn't they have had Supremacy or Conflict? Lots of people liked those.

Still musing, she lifted the lid, took out the folded board and ran her fingers through the dice and tiny houses and hotels. Perhaps Ada was right. Perhaps grown men in prisons did only like Monopoly. She picked out the dice and rattled them in the palm of her hand, then the silver top hat and car and dog, bemused. *Dear Ada.* She tossed the pieces up in the air and caught them, rattled them in her cupped hands, then tossed them up once more, still musing.

'Miss Lyla?'

Lyla turned, feeling guilty to be caught by Solomon in Ada's room, and the pieces fell to the floor.

'Allow me, Miss Lyla,' said Solomon, stepping forward. He bent and picked them up and, about to hand them back to Lyla, said, 'You never knew, did you, Miss Lyla?'

'I never knew *anything*.' She paused. 'I never knew anything, and I never did anything right.'

'You did, Miss Lyla,' Solomon said gently. 'You did *this*. You got this right. It was doing what you did, what you and Lady Ada and Catherine Lively did, night after night, that allowed Captain Spence to escape from the prison in Italy.' He gestured about to the boxes.

Lyla shook her head. 'I don't understand.'

By way of explanation, Solomon held out the little silver top hat and twisted it till it opened. He took Lyla's hand, turning it palm upwards, and tipped the crown of the hat and shook it over Lyla's palm.

Lyla looked down and saw a tiny metal object. Frowning she held it up. *A compass.*

Next, Solomon fiddled with the little motor car and extracted from it a small, sharp metal file.

Lyla frowned. 'I still don't understand.'

Solomon turned and went over to the bookcase.

He pressed a spine, and a section of the case swung open. Slowly Lyla walked forwards. Wads of money held with rubber bands, pots of blue clothes dye, maps, compasses, top hats and dice, silver cars. Lyla's fingers hovered over the wads of money. A little nervously she lifted one down and stared at it.

Reichsmarks? German money, here at Furlongs?

She grabbed another. *Italian lira.*

Suddenly shaking and confused, she held them out to Solomon.

Solomon smiled at her. 'It did the trick.'

Lyla shook her head, still bewildered.

He took from a shelf a larger piece of paper and, unfolding it, handed it to Lyla.

'A map. She'd thought it all through. Maps. Foreign currency. Metal files, Miss Lyla – all to help the prisoners escape, all hidden in these sets.'

Solomon watched Lyla's face as it turned from confusion to gradual understanding and he said, 'It was all for you really, Miss Lyla, for Captain Spence and for you, to bring him back for you . . . He received one of these, miss – a Monopoly set – in a Red Cross box – it made its way to him.'

Lyla gazed at the little silver hat and car and murmured, 'Father . . . Father had one of these?' She looked up at Solomon.

'You didn't get everything wrong, you see,' he said.

'I had no idea . . . All along – no idea at all.'

How had Lyla not known, not imagined what Ada had been about, when she'd been so urgent about the matter of the prisoners? All those evenings, all those boxes, for perhaps a year . . . the frantic sealing and shipping of boxes to Geneva. She smiled to think how a Monopoly set had made its way from the Billiard Room of Furlongs across the channel and all the way across continental Europe to Geneva and finally arrived at the very same remote prison in Northern Italy in which one Lovell Spence was held captive. 'Dear Ada . . . Dear, dear Ada. How clever of her . . .'

'She died knowing, miss, that Captain Spence escaped from the jail in Italy with one of these. There were two other men – She heard they made it home, but that Captain Spence was wounded and separated from them in the Adriatic. She thought it likely he was recaptured, for after that she could find nothing out.'

Lyla nodded. 'Solomon, did Cat know? Did she know all along?'

'I think she guessed, miss.'

Lyla nodded again. *Of course. Of course Cat had known.* She bowed her head.

'I would so have liked her to have been here with me today.'

'She had something to attend to, miss. In London, I believe.' Solomon smiled.

Hearing footsteps on the gravel, then more footsteps in the hall, both Lyla and Solomon turned to the door. Lyla must join the guests. She buttoned her coat and straightened her hat, and Solomon, waiting, held the door open for her.

87

OLD ALFRED

In the Painted Hall beside the coffin stood Prudence and Tawny and Solomon, and on the coffin perched Little Gibson. A little aside from them stood an elderly man, with a serious face and spectacles and walking stick.

Lyla went over to him.

'Dr Gibson, I am so glad you are here.'

He chuckled. 'In a way I was always here, you know –' he touched his heart – 'always close. There was never anyone else.'

Lyla turned and placed on the coffin the photograph that Ada had kept for all these years on her bedside of herself and Dr Gibson when they were young.

Dr Gibson put his stick aside, and he and Tawny and Solomon lifted Ada's coffin on to their shoulders, and Ada was borne out of the house. Lyla followed, and as she stepped outside she gasped, for there on the steps and all around the fountain stood almost every Garden Hill girl who'd ever come to Furlongs.

A guard of honour five girls deep lined the steps and the edges of the forecourt. Lyla searched among them all, looking from face to face, but couldn't find Cat.

Beyond the fountain stood a small group of important-looking men with ribbons and decorations, none of whom Lyla had ever seen before, and beside them stood all the staff of Garden Hill School for Girls and Pinnacle, and beyond them all were lines and lines of motorcars.

Lyla walked slowly between the guard of honour, and as she passed the Garden Hill girls turned and fell into crocodile file behind her. Hand in hand and two by two, they walked across the park, as they'd walked each Sunday up to the chapel at Heaven's Gate. Behind them came the staff and then the guests, and Violet, seeing that everyone was going somewhere, widened her gentle eyes. She swished her tail and lowered her head and followed the procession to the chapel.

Lyla glanced back at Furlongs and saw how Violet's clematis was unseasonably in flower. *For Victory, perhaps, and for Ada.*

Tawny had filled the chapel with the snowy loveliness of Ada's white currants. Lyla was shown to a pew and sat alone at the front of the chapel.

They stood to sing 'He Who Would Valiant Be', but Lyla, for tears, could make no sound come out. A few girls read tributes they'd written. One among them told how Ada believed it essential to keep a carrot always about herself in case she should come across a horse, and how she'd taught the girls to let their minds drift and soar like larks, to dream of all the things that they might do and how they might build their world anew.

A man from the Red Cross talked about Ada's most *vigorous* contribution to the relief of prisoners, and another chap with a beard and a worn tweed overcoat talked of her work as a freelance inventor of experimental weapons, which would, on various alarming occasions, land on the desk of the Secretary of the Armament Design Department. She had drawn inspiration, he said, from the revolutionary mortars used in the Sino-Japanese war, and had concocted her own first mortar from black powder, cigarette papers and a croquet ball. *She was a physicist, botanist and sage*, he said, *with the mind of a projectile missile and the energy of a high-voltage current.*

Pinnacle, too, spoke of Ada – of her verve and gusto, her piercing mind, her unusual approach to mathematics and all other elements of education – and of Pinnacle's gratitude that her girls had been so generously housed at Furlongs. *I cannot say safely housed*, she added, *for nothing about Lady Ada Spence was safe. She'd had the intellect and energy and enterprise of ten generals*, Pinnacle added. *A laugh lovely and loud, a pocketful of gelignite about her person, a heart intrepid and fearless. She was beloved of all that had the fortune to know her.*

Father Scott Talks Rot quite forgot where he was and leaned back against the altar and fumbled for his pipe, and Little Gibson the canary grew melancholy and flew off to hide his sorrow midst the swathes of currant blossom.

Ada was lifted once more and borne out of the chapel, and Lyla followed as they made their way to the spot Aunt Ada had specified for herself.

Must face the old house . . . must have Solomon to hand, keep an eye on you all.

As Ada was lowered into the earth, Lyla saw Solomon in the shadows, limping purposefully from one gravestone to the other, and decided that either grief was affecting him most strangely or that he was up to something.

All of a sudden there was a hissing and a fizzing. At the creeping waft of cordite, the funeral guests glanced uncertainly about the graveyard, then jumped and clutched one another when, from the foot of the ancient yew at the gate, a whooshing firework shot upwards to the skies.

Lyla smiled as a Pink Dandelion bloomed and burst overhead. Everyone's faces turned upwards as it sprouted and sent forth more Dandelions. Lyla turned to Solomon. He smiled at her and bowed as above them and in every corner of the sky the air hissed and crackled and rang as it burst, until fabulous pink showers were falling through all the stars that hung that evening over Heaven's Gate.

Lyla looked on, smiling to think how Great Aunt Ada's lion-taming butler had prepared this tribute to the mistress he had loved, a mistress who would have loved this spectacle.

'Lyla . . .'

Lyla swung round – *Cat*.

'Where have you been?' asked Lyla, her eyes glimmering as all the loneliness and grief of the past few days welled up in her.

Cat smiled. 'Busy. Come on, I want to show you something.'

She held out her hand to Lyla, but Lyla, still full of hurt, looked away. So they walked in silence through the park, and at the lake Lyla paused, remembering all the things they'd done together there at Furlongs over the years and all the fun they'd shared. Yet when she had most needed Cat, Cat had found some other thing that she must do, some other place that she must be.

On the forecourt, Cat took Lyla's hand and smiled. They walked onwards across the gravel to the door. Holding it open for Lyla, Cat whispered, 'You first.' She smiled a smile so full it almost had tears in it.

Lyla stepped inside. She unpinned her hat and placed it on the console table and there, of course, was Old Alfred. Dependable Old Alfred, still, after all these years on his tiptoes; still, after all these years between the Mail In and the Mail Out trays; still watching and seeing and knowing everything.

Yes, he'd known everything, seen everything all along. He'd known the frightened, angry child who'd begged her father not to leave her here, the child who'd tried to run away, the child who'd led a horse upstairs, the child so lonely she'd counted footsteps, sent letters to herself and talked to suits of armour. He'd watched her clod-hop round in shoes a size too big, and watched her linger longingly for the letters that never came, and he'd seen her cast away the letters that she should have read.

He'd known everything all along and always been right, and she herself had got so much wrong.

'Lyla . . .'

Lyla started.

'Lyla . . .'

She slowly turned.

Father. Tall and straight and smiling, thinner, greyer than before, but still *her father*.

'Father!'

'Lyla.'

He swept her up in his arms and for a long while they held each other tightly. Keeping her hands in his, he stepped back a little. Then he drew his hands away from hers, leaving something small in each of Lyla's palms. She looked down and saw a tiny silver top hat in one palm, a tiny silver motor car in the other and burst out, 'They're from here – we sent them – Ada – Ada and Cat and I . . .'

She turned and cast about for Cat, but Father said, 'I know . . . Money, map, compass, file. That's how I got out, Lyla, that's how I survived . . . the reason I'm still here today.'

Lyla could not speak for wonder so Father took her hands again and continued, 'I couldn't write – it was awkward getting home – a little dangerous – I had to take the long way round, so to speak, first the Adriatic, then, after some difficulties, over the mountains, through France, Spain, Gibraltar . . . He found me in a hospital in Gibraltar – your friend's father – and helped me home from there.'

'Cat!' called out Lyla. 'He's here – he's – Father's made it home. It was the boxes – the games – your father!'

At the door stood Lyla's friend.

Lyla saw Cat's shy, proud smile and knew then how large a part Cat had played in all this. That she'd always known why British soldiers held in foreign jails would want to play Monopoly rather than any other game, and she knew too why Cat had kept her company and sat by her side night after night, packing the hundreds, perhaps thousands, of boxes of bootlaces and tinned puddings that would make their lonely, dangerous journey across the channel and over occupied Europe to end up, perhaps, just one of them, in the hands of her friend, Lyla Spence's, father.

ABOUT THE AUTHOR

Sam Angus grew up in Spain. She studied Literature at Trinity College, Cambridge, taught A-level English for a while, designed clothes for a while longer and is now a novelist. She lives between London and Exmoor with an improvident quantity of children, horses and dogs.

THE HOUSE ON HUMMINGBIRD ISLAND

SAM ANGUS

'We're going to a fine place,' Idie told
Homer to console him, 'with gullies and
monkeys and hummingbirds.'

Idie Grace is twelve when she inherits a grand house on
a Caribbean island and is sent away from grey old England
to a place where hummingbirds hover and monkeys
clamber from tree to tree.

As a lady of property Idie can do as she pleases, so she fills the
house with exotic animals, keeps her beloved horse in the
hall and carries a grumpy talking cockatoo called Homer
on her shoulder. But her island home holds as many secrets as
it does animals, and the truth behind Idie's inheritance
is the biggest secret of all . . .